THE
VALDEZ
HORSES

THE VALDEZ HORSES

Lee Hoffman

Thorndike Press • **Chivers Press**
Thorndike, Maine USA   Bath, England

This Large Print edition is published by Thorndike Press, USA and by Chivers Press, England.

Published in 1999 in the U.S. by arrangement with Golden West Literary Agency.

Published in 1999 in the U.K. by arrangement with the author.

U.S. Hardcover 0-7862-2025-2 (Western Series Edition)
U.K. Hardcover 0-7540-3876-9 (Chivers Large Print)
U.K. Softcover 0-7540-3877-7 (Camden Large Print)

The text of this Large Print edition is unabridged.
Other aspects of the book may vary from the original edition.

Set in 16 pt. Plantin by Minnie B. Raven.

Printed in the United States on permanent paper.

British Library Cataloguing in Publication Data available

Library of Congress Cataloging in Publication Data

Hoffman, Lee, 1932–
    The Valdez horses / Lee Hoffman.
        p. (large print) cm.
    ISBN 0-7862-2025-2 (lg. print : hc : alk. paper)
    1. Large type books. I. Title.
    [PS3558.O346V3   1999]
    813′.54—dc21   99-30990

To the Hoffman clan —
Mom and Dad, Doris and Curt,
Gary, Chris and Terry.

I

He gave me a start, sitting there like that on the leggy bay pony, sort of silhouetted against the twilight sky. Partly it was the way he sat, deep and easy in the saddle with his feet out of the stirrups and his legs hanging, and partly it was the horse being rangy and long-legged with the same kind of fine straight line to its head that Flag'd had. It was like seeing a ghost.

Then he called out, "I'm looking for the Wagner spread." It was a kid's voice, a bit shy and uncertain.

"You found it," I answered, not seeing a ghost any more but just a youngun on a long-legged horse. "Light and set."

He stepped down and I could see he was maybe sixteen or so. There was an old bedroll tied back of his cantle and both him and the pony had that dusty, weary look of having been on the trail for a while.

"You hunting for work?" I asked. I recalled mentioning around town how I could use a boy to help out on the place. I figured maybe somebody there had sent him to look for me.

He nodded so I asked him then if he'd run away from home.

"No sir." He sounded a bit embarrassed, but sincere. I guess I'd sounded the same way answering the same question when I was a kid . . . hell, that was around twenty-five years ago. And I'd been lying.

Did kids still run away from home to see the frontier and learn the cowboying trade, I wondered. But the world had changed a lot since I left home back in '75 and that frontier is gone now. The West is settled, civilized and chopped into pieces by long strings of barbed wire. The buffalo herds, the blanket Indians, the wild mustang *manadas,* they've all been tamed or wiped out. And the men — they're different too. Standing there remembering, I felt a kind of emptiness, both for myself and for this kid who'd never see the world I'd seen when I was his age.

I pulled my thoughts back to the present and asked him, "Ever do any ranch work?"

His answer came as a surprise. Usually it's the city kids who head West. The country kids strike out to see the big city when they take a mind to leave home. But this youngun told me, "Yes sir. I was raised up on a ranch. My folks got a little spread on the Mussel-shell. We breed fine horses. Like the one I'm riding." He hooked a thumb over his shoulder at the bay. From the tone of his voice, he was right proud of it.

"What are you doing hunting work around here then?" I asked.

He seemed to be a naturally shy kid. He hemmed a bit, but when he spoke up I had a feeling he was telling me the truth. "My pa always told me there was a whole mess of country this side of the river. So when him and me agreed I was old enough, he gave me an outfit and said I could go ahead and take a look at it."

"Just turned you loose?"

He nodded. "He said I should write now and then and fetch on home if ever I got the notion."

"Sounds like you got a smart pa," I said, thinking as how a boy who's let to go of his own free will is more likely to return of it. I'd never gone back home myself and sometimes I was sorry for that. But I'd never been really sorry I'd left.

The boy grinned a bit and said, "I reckon my pa's about as smart a man as there is. Ain't nobody knows horses better'n him."

I grinned at that myself. As I led him toward the barn I told him, "Used to work on a horse ranch back when I was about your age. It was the first ranch job I had."

I sat myself down on a rail while he pulled the saddle off his bay and started forking it some hay. Next thing I knew, I was telling him all about how I'd left home.

My father'd been killed in the War between the States when I was just a sprat so my mother and sister and I had gone to live with my aunt in Savannah. She had some kind of small income and they added to it by sewing. Soon as I got big enough I was put to working in a drygoods store afternoons after school. And I hated it.

I took good to reading as a kid, and what I read mostly was about the frontier — everything I could get my hands on about it. I begun to plan that someday I'd go out there myself and I started hoarding up the part of my wage that I was let to keep. My aunt said thrift was a virtue in a youngun and started giving me money for my birthdays. Day I turned fifteen she gave me a half-eagle. I decided then I had enough of a stake, if I could travel most of the way by freight train the way I'd heard a lot of men did. First night I got the chance, I stuffed a few belongings into my pockets and went down the drainpipe.

I fell into luck of a sort at the freight yards by running into a feller who was going the same way as me. He called himself Ben Bolt and he showed me how to get onto a train. He taught me a fair bit about traveling that way and we got right friendly. I told him about myself and my ambition and how I'd set my goal on getting to the Yellowstone country. Of all the things I wanted to see, most of all I was eager to set eyes on Colter's Hell. I planned to get there first and then go looking for work. I thought I might take up cowboying or Indian fighting, though I have given some serious thought to finding gold.

Well, I learned a lot from Ben Bolt all right. After a while he tried to steal my money. I got away from him with it and after that I was a lot more suspicious of the strangers I met on freight trains.

I found I could eat regular by exchanging chores for meals at houses along the way. Sometimes I'd lay over in a town for a few days and pick up a little money swamping in stores or helping unload wagons or the like, too. The further west I got the friendlier people seemed to be toward a drifting youngun. Only trouble was the houses kept getting farther and farther apart and sometimes I went a long time between meals. But I kept moving west.

A few times I stopped at ranches and got to spend the night in bunkhouses with real cowboys. I sure heard a mess of stories from

them. Mostly big long windies, but in between they'd sometimes tell true stories
about the range. More than once, listening
to them, I'd decide to put off my trip to the
Yellowstone awhile and take work on a
ranch. But I just couldn't seem to find a
riding job.

I'd had a notion there'd be plenty of work
for a likely boy who was strong and eager
even if he didn't know a beef critter from a
milk cow. But looking back, I reckon there
must have been near as many green kids
wandering around the West in those days as
there were beeves on the range.

Even if I didn't get to try my hand at
cowboying, I did learn a fair bit from listening to the men talk. By the time I reached
Colorado I figured I knew quite a lot. For
one thing, I knew a man had his own outfit
and likely a horse of his own, too. I decided I
was gonna make the rest of my trip astride,
so I counted my money and set out to buy
myself some gear and a horse.

I started with boots and spurs and a
broad-brimmed hat, so I'd look a cowboy
when I went to pick out a horse. They
weren't very fancy and I didn't pay much for
'em. But I didn't have much left either and I
ended up with a bony-hipped old mare and
a tattered hull of a saddle. The stableman

threw in a bedroll of sorts and a ragged old blanket coat somebody'd left a long while back and never come to claim, and I set out, riding north.

By the time I got to the Long Mountains, I hadn't a penny left in my pockets and that mare and I were both gaunting up. I didn't know beans about living off the land and ranch houses were pretty few and far between up that way.

When I rode into Jubilee town I got stopped right off by a feller who set into asking me questions. Turned out he was the sheriff and he'd spotted me for a runaway. He didn't try to send me home, though he offered to telegraph my folks if I wanted to go back. I said no to that, so he listened out my story, bought me a meal, and suggested I head across the Horne River to a beef ranch belonging to a feller name of Gil Nash who might be able to put me on for a while.

It was coming winter then and the sheriff warned me that the Yellowstone was far away and hard traveling once the snows came. He said if Nash couldn't hire me, I should head back and take any kind of work I could find in the town to see me through the spring. I didn't think much of that idea. I had hopes once I'd got my outfit and my horse, I'd seen the last of sweeping out

13

stores, so I was bound and determined I'd get myself hired at this Nash's place. Maybe I would have, too, only I got lost.

It was turning night and getting right cold up there in those slopes and I hadn't seen horn nor hair of a ranch. I'd lost the road back to Jubilee and even the game trail I'd followed by mistake to where I was. I was purely and completely lost.

I sat there in my saddle, huddled up inside that old coat, with my hat pulled down over my ears and my breath frosting up in front of my face. I didn't know what to do, so I just sat staring up at a mess of stars that were like chunks of ice over my head. They threw down a cold white light and as far as I could see there wasn't anything else in the whole world except me and my pony and the stars and ridges.

Then suddenly that old mare gave a snort and started moving along the ridge. Not having any notion where to go myself, I let her have her head and next thing I knew, I seen a light that wasn't a star. It was sitting down in between a couple of ridges and it had the warm yellow color of lamplight.

I laid heels to the mare then and pretty soon I could see I was coming onto some kind of a spread. It wasn't much to look at — just a few plank buildings, some pole corrals and a fenced pasture. But there were horses in the corrals and there was that lamplight in the window of the cabin. That sure made it look good to me.

I rode into the yard, sniffing deep of the scent of woodsmoke and cooking, and started to hello the house. But before I could get my mouth open, the door spilled out a square of that warm yellow light. There was a man silhouetted in the doorway and he called out, "Do I know you?"

It seemed like an odd greeting. He had his head cocked a bit, like he was looking at me, and maybe he could see me in the starlight. But with that lamp behind him the way it was, I couldn't make out his face at all.

"I reckon not," I answered, feeling bashful but awful happy to see another human being. "My name's Jamie Wagner. I — I'm looking for work."

"You sure look in funny places," he muttered. He didn't sound like he welcomed company. But he didn't seem really put out either. He walked over and laid a hand on my pony's chest. "You run away from home?"

"No sir," I answered. I meant to claim I was my own man. But seeing the way he touched the mare, I could feel my face beginning to flush. I hoped he couldn't see it there in the dark. Why'd I have to have a *mare* anyway? I'd heard it said that mares were for breeding, belling or ladies' mounts. It wasn't considered manly for a *feller* to ride one. He'd know for sure I was just a dumb, green kid.

"Climb down if you want. Food's cooking and you can bed here for the night," he said.

I followed him into the cabin. It wasn't anything but a plank shack with a dirt floor and a couple of bunks built up against the walls. There was a table in the middle with some chairs up to it and a chest like a trunk against one wall. But most important to me right then, there was a big iron stove glowing at the firedoor and filling-up the cabin with its warmth.

He walked up to the stove and lifted the lid off the kettle. Glancing into it and sniffing, he nodded to himself. Then he turned toward me.

That was the first I'd seen of his face. I had started to unbutton my coat but I stopped dead when he looked at me.

He was dark-complected with lank black hair and he was kind of small, but built lean and compact like a mustang so you didn't notice his size at first. What you noticed was his face.

In the lamplight his eyes seemed as black

and shiny as obsidian. He had a scar on his forehead that cut down across his right eyebrow. It stopped there and started up again on his cheekbone, curving back toward his ear. It must have been an old scar because it was faded and didn't show much. But it twisted his eyebrow up so that the way he was frowning at me and with those dark eyes he looked like — well, to me right then he looked like the devil himself. And me and him were alone there.

I took a step backward and stammered, "I — I don't think I'd better stay. I gotta be somewhere."

He grinned and it didn't help any at all. The way the scar ran across his cheek, it gave a twist to his grin too. His lip drew up, showing his teeth like a wolf, and his eyes narrowed. I had a shivery feeling that he could look right inside me with those eyes, maybe even pull the soul out of me with them.

He said, "There ain't any *somewhere* around here for you to be."

Swallowing hard, I took another step back. I was against the door. I said, "I gotta get to the Nash ranch."

"You're a long ways from there. Too far to make it tonight. They expecting you?"

I meant to lie and say that they were, but it

stuck in my throat. I just shook my head.

He turned his back to me and as he started reaching stuff down off a shelf, he said, "Nobody eats around here without he's tended his stock. Lamp's by the door and there's hay in the barn."

I wasn't sure what to do, so I did what he told me. I lit the lantern and as I headed out, he called after me, "You set fire to the barn and I'll roast you over the ashes."

I had a feeling he really would, too.

Outside, I just stood as the thoughts churned in my head. It was cold and dark and that food smelled awful good. Finally I went and stripped the saddle off my mare. By the time I'd hayed her, I'd about convinced myself that he wasn't really the devil but only a human same as me. I wasn't quite ready to go back into the cabin with him though, so I walked over to the pasture and looked at the horses in it.

As best I could tell they were young, mostly solid and dark of color. That reminded me how I'd heard that outlaws preferred dark mounts that wouldn't catch the eye too easy. These didn't look like plain old range cowponies, either. They were leggy and fine-headed like running horses.

In my mind I seen those black, evil eyes again and I thought of how strange he'd greeted me. Had I blundered onto an outlaw camp hidden up here in the mountains? Maybe there was a gang out doing robberies and murders right this minute and they'd be riding back soon with their guns still hot from killing. They'd murder me for sure if they found me here.

Maybe they were renegades, I thought. I'd heard some awful bloody stories about renegade whites and half-breed Indians. They say they're worse than any wild blanket Indians. That dark-headed, dark-skinned devil inside the cabin — he might be a 'breed from the look of him. Maybe he meant to feed me and see me bedded and then when I was asleep, he'd cut my throat and lift my scalp.

Well, I sure didn't intend to wait around and find out. I started back toward the corral, meaning to saddle my horse and sneak away, real quiet. But just as I touched hand to my saddle the door of the cabin opened and I heard him holler, "Hey kid, hustle it! Grub's on the table."

It felt like the bottom fell out of my stomach. I stood froze. It was too late to sneak away now. If he was an outlaw he'd sure take off after me if I tried to run. Forcing myself, I turned back.

He gestured me to one of the chairs and I

sat down on the edge of it. There was a plate in front of me, piled with beans and biscuits. It sure smelled good. I decided I might as well eat. But my fingers were a little shaky as I reached for a biscuit. And just then he turned from the stove and looked at me. The biscuit slipped right out of my hand as his eyes met mine.

He forced the grin off his mouth and said, real solemn, "Don't worry. I don't eat kids like you. Not when I got a good side of beef hanging."

I must have blushed clear up to the roots of my hair. It was like he'd seen every thought I'd had.

He tossed steaks out of the frypan into both our plates and then sat down across from me. I guess the joke had begun to wear thin for him because his eyes went serious as he looked at me. At that, the evil seemed to go right out of them. His face wasn't a devil's mask any more. And close up I could see that his eyes weren't really solid black. They were dark brown and kind of velvety, like a horse's.

"I'm Chino Valdez," he said to me. He spoke soft and quiet, like he was talking to a spooky pony. "This here is a horse ranch. I tame broncs but I don't eat kids. If you want, you can spread your blanket in one of the sheds. But it's a damnsite warmer inside here."

I could feel that I was blushing worse, clear down to my knuckles. I surely did feel like a fool. I turned my face down and stared into my plate, knowing he could see just how embarrassed I was. That's the worst thing about being a light-complected redhead. Least thing I felt, it would blaze right up and show all over my face. I gulped and mumbled, "I'm sorry, Mister Valdez."

"Nobody calls me *mister* and damn few *Valdez*," he said as he slashed into his steak with his knife. "I answer to Chino."

He made himself real busy with eating, not paying me any more mind. I was grateful for it.

I started in to eating myself and for a while we neither one of us said anything. Soon as I got a mouthful of that grub I begun to forget everything except how hungry I was. And when I did look up at him again, I didn't spook.

I couldn't help but keep glancing at that scar and the way it twisted his face. I guess he noticed because after a while he said, "Near got stomped by a bronc once. Didn't learn nothing by it though. Still work at the same fool trade. You ever work around horses?"

For a minute I didn't know what to say. I wasn't feeling afraid of him any more and when he said that it suddenly come to me maybe he could use a hired hand. I surely did need a job and I wanted riding work, not some broom-pushing job in town. But I had a feeling it wouldn't do me any good to lie to him about what I knew. Those eyes seen too deep.

I shook my head and set in to telling him a bit about what I'd done since I left home. I tried to make it sound good, like I'd learned a lot when I was crossing the country. But as I listened to myself talk, the hope begun to go out of me. And by the time I was done I felt sure he could see that I wasn't anything but a fool green kid who'd run away from home. I had to own to myself that was all I was.

He didn't say anything to what I'd told him and when I added on as how I just *had* to find work for the winter, he only nodded. I felt pretty disappointed at that. It seemed to me that even if he couldn't hire me on himself he could suggest somewheres I could look for work. Or at least he could say something encouraging. Or something.

The way he didn't say anything at all left me feeling like I was hanging on the end of the last words I'd spoke. As I finished up eating I kept casting back in my mind over what I'd said, wondering if somehow I'd made myself sound like such an idiot-kid that there just wasn't anything he could say to me. The more I thought about it, the lower I felt.

He cleaned off his plate and cocked back his chair, setting his heels up on the table. I seen then that he wasn't wearing the regular high-heeled Mex boots like all the cowboys I'd met had worn. His were of soft leather, folded over and fringed at the tops. There was a lot of fancy beadwork on them, making them look like some kind of Indian stuff. After a minute or two of looking, I realized they weren't boots at all, but high moccasins with knee-high leggings over them. I'd never seen anything like them before.

He built himself a cigarette and then said to me, "That's a mess of dirty dishes, ain't it?"

I nodded in agreement, though it wasn't really very many.

"About twice what I usually have," he added.

I finally got the point. I set into clearing the table and washing up. When I finished, he told me where things belonged on the shelves. He didn't move the whole time, except to stub out the cigarette, and he didn't say anything except where the stuff belonged. But he kept watching me without he looked straight at me and it gave me a funny feeling.

When I'd finished, I stood myself in front of him as if to ask did he want me to do anything else. He looked me over again from head to heels, just barely frowning, the way a man will when he's examining a horse up for sale.

I looked him over, too. He wore a real faded red wool shirt that had been patched up a few times, and snug-legged brown britches. Instead of a belt or galluses, he had a bright red sash around his middle. He wasn't wearing a handgun, but then a lot of fellers don't keep them on indoors. It wasn't till later I learned he didn't have one.

It was the leggings with the beadwork that caught my interest. If I'd had more nerve I would have asked him about them. But his strange quiet manner didn't encourage me any and for all my big thoughts about being a man I really wasn't but just a bashful kid.

He frowned thoughtfully as he studied me over. Giving a shake of his head, he stood up. That was when I realized he wasn't any taller than me. I was a long, gangling kid and with those high-heeled boots I'd bought myself, I could look a fair few growed men straight in the eye. But until then I would have swore he was bigger'n me. Even when he was sitting down he kinda seemed somehow to be towering over me. Truth is, I still had that feeling as he stood up and I faced him, eye to eye.

He hooked his thumb toward one of the bunks and said, "I don't share my blankets with no man. You can take that bed if you're of a mind now to sleep inside here."

II

It seemed like I hadn't but got to sleep good when something started shaking me right back awake again. I got my eyes open and seen by the lamplight that it was Chino. He had his hand on my shoulder and was telling me to wake up and roll out.

"What's the matter?" I mumbled, rubbing at the sleep in my eyes. I seen then that he had his sash and leggings on, and I smelled the fresh-cooking coffee.

"Damn near daylight," he said. "Or are you planning to hibernate all the winter like a bear?"

I grumbled something and crawled from under the buffalo robe he'd give me for cover. Breakfast was the same thing we'd had for supper the night before — beans, biscuits, steak, and coffee. But I sure didn't object to that any.

While we were eating, Chino kept watching me the same way — without exactly ever looking at me but still seeing everything I did. It froze up all my questions somewhere inside my throat so that I didn't say anything except when he spoke to me. He didn't do that much and I got to having that same feeling again that I was hanging onto the end of something not yet finished.

After we were through eating he pointed out the dishes again and I busied myself washing them. I was beginning to feel a lot more at ease by then. The cabin had a warm, cozy feeling about it and now that I was over being afraid of him, I decided I kind of liked Chino Valdez. I'll own I surely was curious about him. He wasn't anything at all like the fellers I'd run onto during my travel across the country.

While I was working at the wreckage, he pulled an old sheepskin coat off a wall peg and shrugged it on. Then he took down a quirt that had been hanging on the peg and slipped the loop around his wrist. It was a long, stiff, braided leather whip and it looked real fierce. The sight of it added onto my curiosity. I couldn't believe anybody'd be cruel enough to beat a horse with a thing like that.

When I finished the dishes I went out to look for him. I couldn't find him and I seen his saddle was gone from the barn so I guessed he'd rode off somewheres. I felt kind of disappointed at that.

Leaning on the corral rail, I gazed at my

mare and thought to myself as how I ought to saddle up and ride on to find this Gil Nash's spread. But I didn't want to leave without I'd seen Chino again. After a while, I went back into the cabin and hunted up things to busy myself with, like sweeping the loose dirt and dust off the hard-packed earth floor and tying up a busted thong in the web of the bunk I'd slept on. Then I built up the fire again and got a pot of coffee cooking. But he still wasn't back.

I set myself down to study over what else I could do around the place to kill time and excuse myself still being there. I was about halfway through a cup of coffee when I heard hoofs outside. I gulped down the rest of the coffee, then grabbed my coat and pulled it on as I headed out the door. I almost walked into Chino coming in.

"Whoa there!" he said, catching me by the arm. "You still here?"

I nodded and he looked past me all around the cabin at the clean-up job I'd done. Pursing his lips kind of critical, he nodded. Then still holding onto my arm, he headed me into the yard. He pointed me out an ax and a mess of wood waiting to be whittled down to stove-size.

I was willing and I wanted to show him so. Maybe when he seen it, he'd offer to hire me on. I pitched right in. I'd just turned to haul another log up onto the chopping stump when he sat himself down on it, right in my way.

He looked at me with his head cocked to one side and he said, "Boy, I can't pay you nothing for the work you're doing around here."

I didn't know what to say to that.

He looked up at the sun overhead. "If you're gonna make Nash's before dark you'd better get moving. It ain't no short sprint from here."

I mumbled, "Got to finish chopping this wood first."

"Can't pay you nothing," he said again. But he got up and walked away, leaving me to work.

I got most of the firewood stacked in the bin by the door and took an armload on into the cabin. I found him there, sitting with his feet on the table and a cup of that fresh-brewed coffee in front of him. He seemed to be studying over some thought and he only glanced at me as I dumped the wood by the stove. I helped myself to some coffee and sat down across from him.

After a couple of minutes, he spoke up. "That mare of yours is a mite gaunted."

I nodded.

"She could do with a bit more rest and feed." He sounded like he was speculating about some thought.

"Yes sir," I said.

"I gotta ride out and bring in a mare. If you want to leave your horse rest a day, I'll lend you a mount and you can come along. I'll show you the *manada*. I got a studhorse the like of which you ain't never seen and you won't never get a chance to see again. You could head on over to Nash's first thing in the morning."

"Yes sir!"

He grinned at me. Finishing off his coffee, he said, "Come on then. I can't waste all day here."

He roped a lineback dun out of the corral and told me, "You take old Buck here. I'll fetch me one of the colts."

While I was putting my saddle onto the buckskin, he got himself a sorrel geld. I was busy and didn't notice much of what he was doing until he climbed on board. Right then the sorrel put its head down and humped its back. It caught my attention as it went straight up into the air, all four legs stiff. Then I stopped and stared.

Chino sat easy in the saddle. And that was all he done. He just sat there, letting that pony buck and twist. After a minute it stopped high-jumping and stood, snorting and trembling. Then he swung down out the saddle and walked to its head. It started, staring at him and tossing its head as he ran his hands all along its neck and down its chest. When he was doing it, he kept talking real soft and slow, and before long the horse stopped trembling. It just watched him sort of curious.

He stepped up to the saddle again. The sorrel started to put its head down, but he held a short rein on the hackamore and ran his free hand out along the horse's neck and kept on talking. Next thing I knew he laid rein along its neck, shifting his weight in the saddle, and that bronc stepped out as nice as you please.

He turned toward me and said, "Ain't you coming?"

That was when I realized I was standing there like a log, just staring. Feeling my face flush again, I set a foot to the stirrup and swung up onto the buckskin. I could feel it go tense under me and I had a sudden thought that it was gonna bust loose the way the sorrel had done.

Chino cocked his head and looked at me critically. "You scared of old Buck?"

"No sir," I said but I didn't sound like I meant it.

"Then ease up on yourself. Long as he's got his head up like that he ain't gonna make you no trouble."

I looked at Buck's head sticking straight in front of his shoulders, and his ears slopping forward kind of lazy-like. I could feel how stiff I was sitting and I tried to relax. I went as limp as I could. Buck just twitched an ear.

"Look here," Chino said. "You ain't a wood Indian and you ain't a sack of flour. And that ain't no dumb-headed stall-kept hack you're on. You don't want to fight him but you don't want him packing you like you was a bedroll neither. He's got good sense and if you act like you ain't, it's gonna worry him. Maybe make him nervous."

I straightened up then, trying to set somewheres between hanging slumped and sitting ramrod stiff. Finally I got myself to a position that suited Chino and we started off.

"If you want to learn to ride," he was saying to me, "what you want is to get a clever pony to mess around with and ride him bareback for a while. Without you've got a saddle between him and you, you can get to understand each other a lot faster."

"A clever pony?" I said.

"I don't mean any green bronc. I mean a

pony that's wise enough to learn you what it's all about. Forking some snuffy bronc ain't nothing much. Plenty of fellers can do it. There ain't so many that can reach an understanding with a green pony so's he don't go all snuffy every time you climb on his back. That happens, you're wasting his time and strength and yours, too. Thing with a horse is . . ." He stopped short and looked over his shoulder.

Buck stopped without I touched the rein and I looked back myself. There was a buggy topping over the ridge and heading down the trail toward the cabin.

"Today Wednesday?" Chino asked me and I nodded. With a disgusted sigh, he muttered, "I purely forgot about that damn buyer."

He headed back to the cabin and I followed along. He sure didn't seem happy about this man coming and I decided I'd likely best stay out of the way. I stopped by the water trough while Chino went on to meet him.

After some talk, Chino went into the pasture with a rope in his hand. He dropped a loop on a bay horse that the buyer pointed out and led it over. The way he roped that horse, well, he just walked toward it and flicked out his hand and the loop was around the horse's neck. It was real pretty to watch.

He twisted the rope into a come-along on the bay's head and then stretched it out a ways. That was when I seen how he used that long quirt. He'd tap at the bay's flank, light and easy, to make him move at the end of the rope. He could use that ugly whip as gentle as the touch of a hand.

I'd climbed down off Buck, meaning to turn him back into the corral, but I got so interested in watching Chino show those horses that I pure forgot about him. I just set a foot up on the water trough, leaned my elbow on my knee and watched.

There wasn't a one of those horses that wasn't handsome in that long-boned, rangy way. Every one was straightfaced and wide between the eyes with his ears perked up lively and intelligent. I could tell they weren't but green-broke and some of them fussed around a lot while Chino showed them. But mostly they behaved real well, standing to let him and the buyer go over their legs and lift their hoofs and look at their teeth.

It took all afternoon what with the buyer studying and shaking his head and sometimes asking to see some of them over again. I could see Chino didn't feel near as patient toward him as he did toward the horses. But finally the buyer settled his mind and Chino coiled the rope and hung it on a pole. Then come the real talking.

From where I was I couldn't hear it, but I could tell Chino wasn't at all happy about what was being said. He'd gesture with his hands and he'd slap that quirt against his leg, each slap getting harder and harder until I figured he must start feeling the sting of it. But he didn't seem to.

When it was all done and they'd agreed the buyer got into his buggy and drove off. Once he was gone, Chino wheeled around, swinging the quirt at a fence post like it was an ax. It snapped hard against the wood and the thong wrapped itself around. He stood there looking at it for a moment before he jerked it loose.

Walking toward me, shaking his head, he muttered, "Railroad delivery! I ain't but one man. How the hell can I drive them horses to town and fetch down the mare both?"

"Can I help?" I asked, real tentative.

He looked hard at me like he was wondering the same thing. "Likely not. I don't need no help droving and you sure couldn't bring the mare in."

He slapped the whip against his leg again and gazed back over the pasture for a while.

Then he straightened his shoulders like he'd decided what had to be done, whether he liked it or not. Turning to me again, he said, "If you want you can strip the saddle off Buck and practice working him around a bit."

Buck wasn't a very big horse and he wasn't much to look at, being kind of stubby and short and thick through the neck, with heavy head and feathered legs. When I'd took the saddle off and studied over him, I decided he didn't look very young and spirited either. I swung astride him and picked up the reins.

He started walking slow and easy like he knew he had a fool green kid on his back and figured he didn't want to bust me. By time we'd circled the buildings I'd got a fair amount of confidence in sitting him without stirrups. I reckon he'd got some too because when I gigged him, he picked up into a running walk. I could feel all the muscles in him flowing under me and I could feel myself responding, my body moving with his. I seen what Chino'd meant when he talked about me and the horse understanding each other. It was like we were river waters, all running together, each a part of the other. Then I lost the rhythm of his stride and begun to bounce.

He stopped short. He almost pitched me over his head doing it. But I got my fingers wrapped tight into his mane and my legs clamped to his sides. I think he almost went to bucking at the way I grabbed onto him. But he only tossed his head and snorted like he was pretty disgusted with me. He stood waiting while I got myself settled again and ungripped his mane. I could feel my face going red and I understood what Chino'd meant about the horse having good sense. When it come to riding, Buck was a lot smarter than me. He'd accepted the notion of me trying to ride and he was willing to learn me what he could. But I'd made a fool of myself to him and I was awful embarrassed by it.

I wanted to get him back into that running walk again but I just couldn't. I touched heels to him and he went to jogging, bouncing me up and down like a sack of beans. When I reined him down to start over, he stopped stockstill. All he'd do for me was jog or stand. I got to feeling more and more of a fool. Finally I let him go to jogging with the notion that I'd best get him back to the corral and give up for the day. By the time I got there though I'd begun to get the feel of that jog trot and I wasn't bouncing so bad any more.

There was a corral gated up against the pasture and when I rode up, Chino was driving horses into it. He'd already cut a dozen head of those green ponies into it and was going after another one. I reined Buck to a halt and sat there watching him.

He was afoot and he stepped in and out among those ponies, talking soft to them all the while. He wheeled and turned as quick afoot as a cutting horse, using his voice and his hands and that quirt to separate the ones he wanted.

He cut three more into the corral and then pulled up the gate rails. Wiping at his face with the back of his hand, he grinned and asked, "Buck learn you anything?"

"He learned me I didn't know as much as I thought I did," I admitted.

"I seen you didn't once come off him. He musta took a liking to you and give you a real easy lesson."

"He's a gentle horse," I mumbled.

"Buck? Gentle? He's just exactly as gentle as he's got it in mind to be — no less. Buck's mustang pure through and he's solid rawhide when he takes a mind to be."

I won't say I disbelieved him but I said, "He rode real gentle for me."

He raised an eyebrow. "Come to think of it, it's been a few years since he showed me the mustard too. You reckon maybe he's settled a mite?"

"I'd sure like to ride him again sometime," I said.

He didn't give me any answer to that. Instead he looked back at the ponies he'd corralled. "You want to go in and get supper started?" he said to me.

Well, it was his food and he was sharing it with me. I dropped off Buck and turned him out and then headed into the cabin. I was ready to throw the steaks into the pan when Chino finally came along.

We ate quiet again. Afterward, I set in to clearing up. I had a notion he was pleased to see me fall to it, though he sure didn't give me any sign. He acted like it was the most natural thing in the world for me to be there washing the dishes.

Once I was finished and had settled myself, he asked me, "You leaving for Nash's in the morning?"

I'd been thinking on that and had my answer all ready. "I kinda thought I might go back to Jubilee."

Likely he seen easy enough what I was hoping. He said, "I reckon you're planning to ride down with me and the horses then?"

I nodded.

He didn't say anything else. But after a

while he got up and stretched. With a yawn, he told me, "We'd better bed down early if we mean to get them horses into town on time."

I laid there in my bunk awhile before I fell asleep, thinking how he'd said *we* and wondering if maybe he was beginning to consider hiring me on. If he didn't say something about it before long, I meant to ask him outright.

III

We were up before dawn again. By the time the sun topped the ridges, we had the chores finished. Chino'd chose to ride Buck and by the time I got my saddle on my mare, he was mounted up waiting for me. He sat deep and easy into the saddle, with his legs loose and his feet out of the stirrups.

As I rode over, he looked at me critically and said, "I don't reckon you're gonna be no help but I'd be obliged if you don't hinder me none."

That hurt and I was real determined I'd be as much help as I could. Only before long I realized I just didn't know how. And he didn't need any more help than that buckskin horse was.

It seemed like Buck did all the work. The bunch tended to stay together and when one or another would start to drift or lag, Buck would be right there working it back into the bunch without a sign I could see from Chino.

I just strung along behind them.

We didn't move very fast and it was late

41

afternoon by the time we sighted the town. Chino herded the horses right down the main street. There was a back way he could have gone but I think he wanted folks to see his horses.

It was when he got to the holding pens by the railroad I finally got to do something. A bay geld decided not to go in and wheeled off. I swung my mare and headed him back just as Chino came up to me on Buck. He moved on in and took over and pushed the bay on in. He never said a thing to me about my helping.

Once they were penned, he settled himself on a fence rail and rolled a smoke. I hung around a while, waiting for him to say something. When he didn't, I climbed up and set next to him. He didn't even look at me.

In a while the horse buyer come walking down the road. Him and Chino looked over the horses again and then headed toward the main street together. I followed along a couple of paces back like I just happened to be going the same way. When they started up an outside staircase I stopped across the street and waited, watching them.

Chino banged on the door a couple of times but there wasn't any answer. He looked annoyed about that. Taking a pencil and a tallybook out of his pocket, he wrote something and gave it to the buyer. He got back a wad of paper money. Once he'd licked his thumb and counted it over, he shook hands with the buyer and they came back down the stairs.

The buyer trotted off and Chino paused, looking across the street at me. He stuffed the money into his shirt pocket and strode toward me.

"Come on," he said, like he'd been expecting me to wait for him. I hadn't any notion where we were going, but I followed.

He walked into the sheriff's office. I stopped in the doorway. The sheriff was sitting behind his desk. He glanced at me, then said sociably, "Howdy, Chino. What you got there?"

He meant me.

"Stray I found on my range."

"Planning on keeping him?"

"Hell, you know I can't afford no hired help."

The sheriff frowned and said, "You're gonna penny-pinch yourself into an early grave, Chino."

Well, he nodded like he agreed. But what he said was, "Lamar, I sold some stock but Stanhope ain't in his office."

"No, he's closed down for a few days. His daughter's back home now."

"Oh? Then maybe you'll hold this for me till morning?" He reached the wad of bills out of his pocket, peeled one off and held out the rest.

The sheriff eyed the bill he'd held back. "Gonna stay in town tonight?"

"Yeah, I reckon so. I'm tired, Lamar. And I'm thirsty as hell."

The sheriff didn't look very happy. "Don't make no trouble, Chino."

"I'll do my best," he answered, taking the receipt the sheriff wrote out.

"Y'know, you're a damned nuisance."

He grinned sort of self-consciously. "Least I don't come into town often."

"Town couldn't take it. Neither could you." The sheriff gave a little grunt and glanced at me again. "Chino, why don't you get yourself some help up to that place? Least that way when you get yourself stomped there'll be somebody around to gather up the pieces."

I caught my breath, hoping he'd take the hint and say something encouraging. But all he answered was, "Time comes I get that stomped, I ain't gonna worry about the pieces."

He left then and I followed along at his side. Finally I got up my nerve and said, "You could hire on a boy real cheap."

44

"No," he grunted, making it sound like the last thing he intended to say on the subject. Pausing, he looked around. We were right across from the cafe and he fingered at that banknote in his pocket. "Well, you done all right not getting in my way," he muttered. "Come on and I'll stand you to a decent meal."

We ate quiet again. It seemed like he had things on his mind and I didn't interrupt his thinking. I was feeling pretty bashful and discouraged. After dinner, we collected our horses from the stock pens and I kept on following as he rode over to the livery stable. The feller there knew him and greeted him real friendly. He said he'd seen the bunch we drove in and spoke highly of them. Chino agreed and then said he'd turn Buck into the corral himself.

"What about that one? He with you?" the stableman asked, nodding toward where I sat my mare, waiting.

Chino looked at me like he hadn't even known I was there. He gave a real deep sigh. "I 'spose you'd better take care of his horse. And bed *him* in the loft tonight. He's riding up to Nash's place in the morning. See he gets off in the right direction, will you?"

He handed the man a couple of coins and walked off. There was no question in my mind he was leaving me there.

After I'd turned out my mare, I spread my blankets in the loft but I wasn't ready to sleep yet so I climbed back down and wandered around town with my hands stuck in my pockets, just looking into windows and such. I was feeling pretty lonesome and hoping awful hard I'd run into Chino and he'd let me tag along with him some more. I didn't though and eventually I went back and bedded down.

The stableman wakened me at sunup and offered me some coffee from the pot he kept cooking. We sat together awhile with me sipping slow to make the coffee last on account I wasn't in any hurry to get to Nash's any more. I got to asking him did he know Chino very well.

" 'Bout as well as most," he said. "He ain't *un*friendly but he ain't exactly sociable. You seen that studhorse of his?"

I shook my head.

"Too bad," he muttered. "That's one fine piece of horseflesh. Them colts he's breeding are fair fine animals too."

Then he got to telling me how Chino'd come into Jubilee with nothing to his name but the Buckskin and the studhorse and had gone into partnership with this Buell Stanhope feller on the ranch. Stanhope wasn't

46

any horseman or a rancher neither one, but he had money and he liked to invest in things.

Chino'd had the idea to build a *manada* of the best Western-type horses he could get hold of, breeding them to the stud, Flag. He aimed for crossbreeds with Flag's fine blood and the ruggedness and good using qualities of the Western stock. It had been fair hard getting the ranch established with all expenses and no return the first couple of years. But now he'd begun to sell greenbroke young horses and a few made using horses and it looked like his plans were gonna work out just fine.

Chino had a way with horses the like of which he'd never seen before, the old man told me. That got me feeling even worse about the way he'd sent me off. I had it in my head I wanted to stay at that ranch and learn about horses. I asked the stableman, "Don't he never hire no help up there?"

"Come time to cut and brand the colts, Stanhope sends him some help out." he answered. "Rest of the year he handles things himself."

"It must be a real job of work to run a place like that alone," I said.

He nodded. "Never in my life seen a man as tightfisted with a dollar as Chino Valdez, excepting when he's drunk. He's a completely different feller then. But sober he don't spend a red cent he don't have to. Year before last he busted a leg messing around with them horses and Stanhope tried to send him some help. He wouldn't hear of it. Said as long as he could stride a horse he didn't need no help. Reckon he didn't neither, though God knows how he got along."

I swallowed the dregs of my coffee and went on out to the corral to catch my horse. That old man sure hadn't encouraged me none, but when I got to thinking how Chino'd bought me a meal and paid my keep for the night, I decided he couldn't be all as stingy as the stableman made out.

Buck was still in the corral so I took my time checking over my gear and rubbing down my mare before I saddled her. But there wasn't any sign of Chino. I'd run out of ways to stall and was just plain standing waiting when he finally showed up.

He had his hat pulled low over his face and his head down and he was walking slow and weary. He shot me a quick look but he didn't say anything. He just saddled up and rode off.

When I climbed on my mare and reined up beside him, he gave me another quick glance and asked, "Where you think you're going?" His voice was harsh and deep down in his throat and his eyes had that real mean look to them again.

I mumbled, "Hunting for work."

"You can ride as far as the fork with me," he grunted.

I didn't say anything else. It was easy to see he didn't want me to. He rode along with his head down, keeping Buck at a walk and seeming to make an outright point of ignoring me.

The fork he was talking about was just past the edge of town. He stopped and without even looking at me he said, "You keep going straight till you come to the river. Cross over and foller the bank to your right. When the wagon tracks turn, stay with 'em. You'll spot the Nash place without no trouble." Then he turned up the side road without so much as a glance back at me.

I sat there, watching his back and wishing he'd — well, he could have invited me to stop by the ranch sometime. At least he could have said goodbye.

He only rode a short way. Then he halted and looked back over his shoulder. "I reckon I promised to show you Flag, didn't I?"

I nodded.

"All right," he said. "I got to get the mare in tomorrow and you can come along. But the morning after, you *got* to get, you understand?"

Eagerly I laid heels to my pony. She jumped toward him. At that Buck gave a snort and started dancing like he wanted to make a race of it. But Chino jerked rein.

"Whoa!" he said to me, real hard. "You hold that horse quiet. I don't feel like no games today."

I hauled my mare steady and we started off at an easy walk. "Where we going?" I asked.

"Stanhope's."

"He's your pardner, ain't he?"

He looked sidewise at me. "Where'd you hear that?"

I admitted, "That stableman told me."

"He tell you anything else about me?"

"Not much," I mumbled.

"Anything you want to know that he didn't tell you?" he asked gruffly. The way he said it, I sure felt ashamed of having asked into his business. I just gulped and shook my head

In a minute or two we come onto Stanhope's place. It was a big two-storied house with porches all around and curtains in the windows. Off to one side was a barn and I saw a couple of nice-looking harness hacks grazing in the field.

Chino told me to wait while he tended his business with Stanhope. He stalked up the steps and rapped his knuckles on the door. While he waited he kept shifting his weight from one foot to the other like he wasn't very happy about being there.

It was a young woman who opened the door. Chino jumped at the sight of her. He took a step back, looking like he was gonna shy and bolt. But then they said some words and he went into the house with her.

It didn't take very long. In a few minutes he came out again with a man behind him. I reckoned it was Buell Stanhope.

"I'll bring Louise over to pick out a horse in a day or two. You have some good ones bunched."

"Ain't gonna be around for a day or two. Got to bring in the mare," Chino answered.

Stanhope looked put out. "You'll be back, won't you?"

"I reckon," Chino grunted as he crossed the porch. He was still walking tired but when he came up to Buck, he swung on without touching the stirrups. Putting heels to the horse, he wheeled and trotted off like he was in a hurry to be away. I lit right out after him and as I came up alongside, he

51

looked at me. This time he grinned.

"That sure was a fair handsome filly, wasn't she?"

I thought back to the pair of harness hacks. They'd looked trim enough, but nothing special. I said as much and Chino laughed out loud.

I knew I'd made a fool of myself again though I couldn't figure quite how. But the way Chino laughed was so good-natured and amused that I didn't mind it much. I laughed too, like sharing the joke, even if I didn't know what it was.

"I mean that daughter of Stanhope's," he told me.

"The girl who answered the door?"

He nodded. "Wouldn't have thought a rank old stud like Buell coulda throwed as pretty a filly as that."

From the look I'd got, she didn't seem like nothing special. I mean she looked about like most of the girls I'd seen in the big towns. She had her hair all done up in curls and her face was pale from being hid under a bonnet. She put me in mind of my sister, who's three years older'n me but silly and flighty and all the time giggling.

"You ever seen anything like her before?" Chino said to me.

"I never paid much mind to wimmen," I

mumbled. "I got more important things to think on."

"Have you?" He looked sidewise at me again, still grinning. He sounded kinda skeptical.

"Ain't you?" I asked.

"Sure. Only that don't stop me thinking on wimmen. Maybe when you've got on toward my age, you'll begin to feel a mite different about it."

I was pretty sure then that I knew my own mind and I answered him real firm, "No sir! I ain't never gonna get mixed up with wimmenfolk."

"I reckon I've said that myself a time or two," he said. "If I'd stayed to it, I'd have saved myself a mess of troubles. Only what a man means to do and what he does ain't always the same thing."

He fell quiet again after that and by the time we reached the ranch his shoulders had slumped down and he looked bone-tired again. When he stepped off Buck he handed me the reins and said, "Here. Make yourself useful and tend the horses. See the stock in the corrals gets hayed, too, will you?"

He tromped off toward the cabin while I got busy with the horses. When I finished and went inside I found him sprawled out on top his bunk sound asleep.

I waited a while, but he didn't waken of himself and I decided I'd best not bother him so I made me a meal of cold biscuits and molasses. He still hadn't wakened when I bedded down for the night.

IV

Before we left out the next morning Chino asked me if I was real sincere about learning to ride and I said I was so he told me to take Buck and ride without a saddle. He took that same sorrel he'd rode before and Buck went alongside, not giving any trouble at all. Before we'd gone very far I began to relax and feel more at ease astride Buck and he began to answer my rein instead of just following the sorrel.

"What's this mare you're after?" I asked Chino, wondering if I might be able to help him somehow.

"Brood mare," he answered. "She's carrying a late foal and I want to bring her up to the cabin before she drops it."

"Do you do that with all the mares?"

"Hell no. It's just that this old lady is something special. I'm hoping she'll drop me a he-colt. What I'm running here now is just one bunch with Flag as the only stud. I want to get a good he-colt to raise up for a second stallion so's I can build a bigger herd. Got to be Flag's blood though and this mare ought to make a good foal for me. Way I figure, by time he's old enough I'll have regular help and be able to handle two bunches."

"Is she a mustang?" I asked.

"Pure through. All iron and guts and shaped up like a Barb," he told me. "Flag though, he's a fancy Eastern-bred. His momma come from Virginia and his grandpa come over from England on a ship. I got a mess of papers for him longer'n the begats."

"How'd you get him?"

"Feller I worked for brought his momma from back East for a brood mare. She was carrying and I was there when she dropped. First time I seen that little he-colt rise up on them skinny legs I knowed he was the horse I wanted. But that damnfool meant to cut him for riding. Hell, he wasn't never intended to wear no saddle. It took me a lot of jawing to convince the old man of that though. And it took me better'n two years to work off paying for him."

We'd pushed on downvalley a good ways and suddenly he halted and pointed off toward a ridge. Softly, he said, "Yonder. There he is."

Well, I'd heard a fair lot of whoppers about horses during my travel out but when

I seen that stallion standing there on that ridge, tossing his head and drinking the wind, I knew nothing Chino'd said about him was a yarn. That was just about the finest thing I'd ever seen in my life.

He was a bigger horse than any of the wild ponies and he had a different line to him, more like the fine-blooded saddlers I'd seen back East. But none of them had the look of Flag. His face was straight and there wasn't much arch to his neck. His legs were long and he wasn't very close-coupled. He didn't have a very thick mess of mane and tail hair either. But he had a look of being strong and solid with a sleek ranginess about him. His color was blood bay with strong black points and not a speck of white on his legs.

I've seen a lot of horses that might have made *prettier* pictures than him but never one that — well, I can't quite explain it except that there was a quality about Flag like he wasn't for decoration but like every muscle and every bone and every hair of him was meant for the business of being a horse.

He stood there for maybe a minute. Then, with a toss of his head, he wheeled and disappeared behind the ridge.

"He's got the mares bunched back there," Chino said. "You're gonna have to wait here. I'm taking Buck now."

I slid down off the horse, but I asked him, "Why can't I ride along? I won't get in the way."

"Flag and his old ladies know me. They ain't wild but they're kinda shy of strangers. They get a good whiff of you, they'll likely light out." He handed me the reins of the sorrel and gestured upslope. "You ride on up to that ridge, you'll probably be able to see them."

I stood watching him ride off. I'd seen how that sorrel acted when Chino mounted up and I wasn't sure I could handle him. But I surely did want to see the *manada*. Finally I got up my courage and set a foot into the stirrup.

Chino'd rode most of the kinks out of the sorrel but there were a couple left for me. He arched his back and the saddle rose to meet me, coming up hard. I bounced a couple of times before I found myself sitting on the ground.

I still had hold of the reins and the sorrel was calmed enough he hadn't gotten away from me, so I decided to try again. Remembering the way Chino'd talked to him, I tried that. I started in telling him what a fine horse he was and how he didn't really want to go throwing me around that way, and I ran my hands over his neck and chest. I could feel him quiver at the touch and then begin to settle.

After a few minutes of that he was standing steady again so I tried climbing up. This time I moved slow and talked soft to him all the while. I managed to get my seat into the saddle before he put his head down and humped and I didn't rise so far on the first bounce. Of course he wasn't humping as hard either which is how come I still had a leg on each side of him when he stopped it and broke into a trot.

By the time I'd managed to get settled down into the saddle and he was answering my rein, we were a fair ways from the place Chino'd left me. I got him turned and headed back and then I seen Chino coming down a ridge riding at an angle to me. He didn't have any mare with him.

I hurried over to meet him, so curious that I almost forgot the way the sorrel acted. I hardly noticed he was fussing and dancing under me until I drew up at Chino's side and the fool horse gave a sudden buck that almost pitched me. I grabbed the apple and even as I got hold of it, I was thinking how I'd made a fool of myself again.

Chino looked me down critically. In a slow drawl, he said, "You know, if a man had the time to take the trouble, he might could make a fair decent rider out of you."

That struck me as about as high a piece of praise as he was likely to speak. I grinned so broad I could feel my ears bending.

With a shake of his head, he told me, "I'm gonna have to backtrack the mare. She ain't with the herd. Could be she come on her time early."

"Is that bad?"

"It could be."

We rode quite a ways before we found her. She was in the grass by a little creek up on the edge of the woods and she was down, lying on her side with her ribs heaving and her neck arched. She kept tossing her head and biting at her flanks.

At the sight of her, Chino stopped the sorrel short and halted me. As he stepped down he told me to hold the horses where we were, and he started toward the mare afoot.

I sat there, trying to see what he was doing, only I couldn't make it out. He kept working an awful long time. The mare struggled and bit at her flanks and tried to nip him a few times. When she finally put her head down it looked like she was too exhausted to keep on struggling.

It was a long while later that Chino rose up to his feet. He had a fuzzy lump in his arms, with four skinny legs sticking out of it in every direction.

He set the foal on the grass, near the mare's head, and she lifted up enough to nuzzle it. Then she laid her head down again and I could see her ribs rise and fall with slow deep breathing. Chino started pulling handsful of grass and rubbing at the fuzzy lump.

I wanted something awful to be over there. I called out softly, "Chino?"

He looked at me then and grinned. "Tie the sorrel and come on over."

As I came up the foal got a couple of its long grasshopper legs squared away and raised up its front end. It tottered a minute and then its hind end come up. But right away its front end went down again. The hind end followed and he lay there in a sprawled heap, catching his breath.

I hunkered next to Chino and asked, "Is he all right?"

"He's just fine!" he answered, grinning at the foal as it made another try at getting all that mess of legs straightened out. Finally the little feller got himself up with a leg at each corner, all splayed out to hold him up. He tried taking a step and it looked like he was gonna trip on his own feet, but he didn't and after a couple of tries, he had the legs

61

working after a fashion.

Taking hold of the foal's head, Chino breathed into its nostrils and then said, "You know me now, feller?"

As he let go, the foal reached out and nuzzled his cheek curiously. He held stock-still while the foal examined over his face and then butted him with its forehead. Then he bent to the mare and tried to move her leg.

She made to kick at him but she didn't have the strength for it. He took hold and pulled her leg up onto his shoulder, using his back to separate her thighs and his hands to guide the foal in. It found her bag all right and in a minute it'd gotten itself a good bellyful of milk and had its legs working pretty well, too. It raised up its head and butted Chino again, this time in the chest.

He eased from under the mare's leg and gave the foal a shove with his forehead, like it was a game he could play too. They played with each other a bit, the foal sniffing Chino all over and nibbling at his shirt, and him scratching its head and rubbing its sides and legs. Then it stopped and begun to fold up its legs, with knees sticking out all over the place. It got itself down, stretched out its head against his thigh and fell asleep.

"He acts like he thinks you're his momma," I said.

"Reckon maybe I'm gonna have to be," he answered, keeping his voice low like he didn't want to wake the little feller. "She ain't gonna last out the night."

"What's the matter with her?"

"She had an accident or something. Maybe fell down. She was a mite lame when I got her. Whatever it was, it started her to deliver and she wasn't carrying him right. I had to turn him for her." He held up his hands and for the first time, I realized he was smeared with blood to the elbows.

He got to his feet and glanced around, like he was looking for something. As he walked toward our mounts, he swung the quirt against his leg. Suddenly he struck out with it, wrapping it around the trunk of a sapling. "Dammit, if I'd got to her sooner . . ." he mumbled. Then he said to me, "We got to find him a momma as can feed him."

"One of the other mares?" I asked.

"There's some with the herd that are still fresh, but ain't none of them old ladies would take too-kind to the idea," he said. He studied the sleeping foal for a long moment. "Hell, he don't need his own momma no more'n I did. We can feed him out an airtight."

"Huh?"

"Sure. That Borden's milk is good stuff.

And if he don't seem to take to it, I can fetch up a wet mare to nurse him."

He wakened the foal and then lifted the mare's leg so it could feed again. When it was satisfied it began to frisk around. It had its legs working a lot better and was finding out how to trot.

Chino walked over to our mounts. He came back leading Buck and carrying the Winchester out of his saddle boot. The foal rushed up to Buck and nosed around his belly. The old geld just arched his neck around to study the youngun. It looked like the two of them decided to be friends.

The foal butted Buck and started looking for teats. He couldn't get it through his baby-head that there weren't any. But Buck didn't seem to mind. I guess he'd been around younguns before.

Chino left them stand together and went back to the mare. He hunkered and scratched her ears. Then he put the muzzle of the Winchester to her forehead and triggered it.

The shot sounded awful loud. It gave the foal a start. He trotted a quick circle around to the far side of Buck and looked out from under his neck to see what was happening.

Standing with the gun hooked over his arm, Chino gazed down at the mare. Slowly, he said, "It's killed meat and it's a good hide. Damn shame to waste it."

"Huh?" The idea shocked me.

"Don't seem right though," he muttered. Then, like it was the most important consideration, he said, "Hell, I ain't got the time to butcher nor the way to pack the meat back. That sorrel wouldn't stand for it."

He handed the rifle to me and went back to the foal. After he'd played with it a while more, he breathed into its nostrils again. Then he gathered Buck's reins and turned toward me. "I reckon we'd better get going now," he said. "You ride the sorrel back and keep him in hand. Don't let him come too near to the youngun."

We rode a ways at a slow walk, with the foal following alongside like Buck was his momma, but after a while the little feller begun to tire out. Finally Chino climbed down and gathered it up in his arms. It was a bit of a struggle for him, getting that foal with all its wiggling legs settled and then getting back onto Buck without a saddle, but he done it. He left the knotted reins lie on Buck's neck and I guess he guided him with his legs because he used both arms to hold the foal across the horse's withers. Me, I was busy with both hands trying to keep the sorrel from acting up.

The sky was almost black and beginning to fleck up with stars when we reached the cabin. Chino headed inside with the foal, leaving me to tend the mounts and the corralled stock. When I finished up and went into the cabin I found he had a fire going in the stove and was messing around with a can of condensed milk and a soft bit of buckskin, making a bag to feed the foal.

He got it rigged and hunkered down, holding the foal's neck clamped under one arm. He put the skin to its muzzle, squeezing a drop of milk through the hole he'd put in it, and got the foal to take a taste. Once that was done, the little feller begun to get the idea and before long he was sucking at the bag as happy as could be.

"What do you think of Banner?" Chino asked me.

"Huh?"

"For a name," he explained. "Little feller's got to have a name and it was Flag sired him. What about calling him Banner?"

It sounded like a fine name to me and I said so.

"Banner it is," Chino nodded. After a moment he let go of the foal's neck and it stood still, sucking away. He looked at me again, "You see? He don't need no more momma than that."

"You don't want him to have no more momma than that," I said. "You want to momma him yourself."

He kind of grinned and answered, "Maybe so. Ain't no reason I can't hand-raise him neither. But you go saying anything like that about me to anybody else and I'll clip your ears off at the roots."

Just then the foal let go the sack and rammed its head into his chest so hard it almost knocked him over. "Whoa, there, Banner," he laughed as he grabbed out with his free hand. "That ain't no way to treat your momma."

He shoved the foal right back and got to his feet. Glancing toward me, he said, "How about you start supper? Us mommas have got to eat, too."

V

Come morning I figured Chino was gonna send me off the way he'd said he would. But I didn't plan on leaving till he chased me. I busied myself with the breakfast wreckage and then some other chores while he messed around with the foal. He fed him and played with him, and when he started out of the cabin, Banner set out at his side frisking like a puppy.

It seemed like maybe Chino'd forgot about running me off. He'd speak to me now and then, telling me to tend to something or just saying to look at how the foal was carrying on, real proud-like.

After a while, he put Banner into the corral with Buck. The foal sure didn't like that any. He'd decided his place was with Chino and he wasn't gonna hear of anything different. He paced along the rails trying to find a way out. When he seen there wasn't any way, he leaned back his head and tried nickering. He made such a funny, pitiful little sound that Chino went back and rubbed his head and played with him a little while longer. Then he told the colt real firm how there was work to be done. That didn't make Banner any difference though. As Chino walked off he kept right on crying.

There were some young horses in the big corral and Chino called me over there. He pulled down the rails between it and the pen and told me to stand by. He meant to cut a gray geld into the pen and when it was there I was to shove the rails back before it could run out again.

I was sure Chino could have separated the horse easy enough by himself, but he was giving me a chance to help and I was real eager to do it. I stood ready while he went in afoot, swinging the quirt and heading for the gray.

It was a fair big horse, built heavier than the others, but it was plenty quick. It would wheel and spin, baring long yellow teeth at Chino. But he got it separated and drove into the pen and I swung the rails into place. When that was done and he'd caught his breath, he took a throw rope and went on into the pen with it.

He forefooted that gray pretty as you please and got a hackamore onto its head. He snubbed the mecate up tight to the post in the middle of the corral and then used that wide sash he wore to blindfold the horse. That calmed the critter down quite a bit and he was able get his saddle on without he had to tie up a leg.

"When I mount up, you pull the gate open," he said to me.

"Are you gonna ride him out?" I asked. It sure looked like a mean horse.

"Gonna run some of the ginger out of him," he said as he jerked up the cinchas. "It's a damnsite easier on him and me both if he runs instead of bucking. 'Sides, this devil's already throwed me once and if I let him do it again, he's liable to get the notion he can do it every time."

He untied the mecate and as he reached for a stirrup the gray heaved out a hind hoof, trying to catch him. Instead it got a lick of his quirt across its haunches hard enough to sting. Chino waited a moment and then stepped up. The gray sure didn't like the idea. As soon as Chino jerked off the blindfold, that horse went straight up into the air in a mess of twisting a whole lot worse than anything I'd seen the sorrel do.

Chino got its head up, though, and aimed it toward the gate. Using his quirt, he broke the horse into a bounding run and off they went. A minute later I'd lost sight of them behind the ridges.

It was a long time before they came back,

but when they did the gray was lathered under the reins and around the saddle and walking instead of running. It shook its head and danced its hoofs, but it answered his hand on the reins.

He kept the horse walking for a while, circling the corrals. Then he rode back into the pen and climbed down. Holding the bosal tight with one hand, he jerked loose the cinchas with the other. When he'd swung the saddle over his shoulder, he slipped the hackamore off and started toward the gate.

The gray stood for a moment shaking its head. Then it lunged. I shouted as I seen it.

Chino started to turn but the horse's bared teeth caught at the back of his shoulder. He hollered, dropping the saddle, and the horse jerked back. It threw up its head, a piece of Chino's red shirt flagging between its teeth. Chino ducked as it went up on its hind legs, both forehoofs striking out. He wheeled away from those hoofs, at the same time swinging the quirt. He swung hard. It striped across the gray's chest, leaving a long thin streak of blood.

The horse squealed as Chino struck out again. For a moment it hesitated, pawing at the air, panicked by the sharp cut of the whip. Then it dropped its hoofs to the ground in a whirl to flee. But Chino's whip caught it across the face, drawing blood again. The horse jumped sidewise, and he lashed out at it with the whip. He drove at it, forcing it back against the fence. It wasn't fighting now but trying to run, trying to escape him. But he kept driving after it, flailing with the quirt.

It scared me, the way he drove after that horse, like he meant to beat it down. I hollered out, "Chino!"

He heard me and stopped short. The horse in front of him was pressed up against the fence rails, trembling and snorting. Keeping his eyes on the animal, he sidestepped toward the edge of the corral. As he ducked out between the rails I could see the back was near ripped out of his shirt.

He walked toward me, wiping at his forehead with the back of his hand. I seen that his face was damp with sweat and real pale. He looked at me hard, his eyes narrow and black and mean. Then he rubbed his knuckles across his face again and mumbled in a harsh voice, "Come'ere."

I started after him as he turned toward the cabin. That was when I seen there was blood on his back. A lot of it. The horse's teeth had taken a chunk, skin and meat, out of his shoulder. He shoved on through the door and sat himself down on the edge of his bunk. Leaning his elbow on his knee, he rested his face in his hand. I could see it hurt him worse than he was willing to own. He sat that way a minute, drawing deep slow breaths. Then he looked up at me. Some of the color had come back into his face and his voice was softer as he said, "Put some water on to boil, will you?"

There were live coals in the stove and I threw in kindling and some firewood. Then I dippered the kettle full of fresh water and set it to heat.

"There's salt on the shelf and muslin in the trunk," he said, so I reached down the sack of salt and got a big piece of sheeting out of the chest. There'd already been pieces torn out of it sometime before. I tore some more and poured the boiling water into a basin with a handful of salt, the way he told me.

When he started unbuttoning his shirt, I made a move to help him, but he shook his head and jerked it off himself. The wound was right ugly. Remembering something I'd heard somewhere, I said, "That ought to be washed out with whiskey. If you've got some, I'll do it for you."

"No!" he snapped at me. "I don't keep no likker around here. And you don't never bring none neither, you hear?"

I nodded and went about washing the wound with the hot salt water the way he told me. As fast as I'd wipe it clean, it'd seep full of blood again, but he said as long as the blood didn't spurt or flood it was all right.

When I'd finished washing and bandaging it I got us both some coffee. By then I think I needed it worse than he did.

He picked up the shirt and held it out so's he could look through the hole in the back. Shaking his head, he said, "You reckon that horse et the rest of my shirt?"

"He dropped it in the corral," I mumbled.

Studying over it, he said, "Maybe I can find the piece and patch it back in." Then he jerked up his head and jumped up. "I dropped my saddle too!"

As he wheeled for the door, I hurried after him. The horse backed off, snorting and looking white-eyed at him when he ducked through the rails. Not paying it any mind, he grabbed his saddle and slung it up onto the fence. It was a double-cinched Mother Hubbard and the mochila showed some fresh scars like the horse had pawed at it. But the tree was sound and that was a relief to him. When he'd made sure of it, he turned back and dug that rag the horse'd torn from his shirt out of the dust. I wondered if he really did have a notion to patch

74

it together again. Sure didn't seem to me it'd be worth the trouble.

All the while that horse stood off against the far fence, quivering with fear as it stared at him. The dried blood was streaked over its face and chest where his quirt had struck. Used hard, that whip could cut like a knife.

Looking at the horse, Chino shook his head slowly and said, "That there gray and me ain't never got along worth a damn."

I recalled bunkhouse stories I'd heard about mean ones and the men who broke them. I asked, "Are you gonna *bust* him?"

"No."

I guess I showed my disappointment in my face because he added, "I could easy enough, if I wanted. There ain't no horse on four legs I couldn't bust if I set in to do the job. But I ain't got to prove it. Not to you nor him nor myself neither. Not no more."

I didn't say anything and after a moment he asked me, "You know what it is, *busting* a horse?"

"You show him you can't be throwed, don't you?" I said and as I said it I had a feeling it was wrong.

"Busting a horse is just exactly that. You *bust* him — break him down. I've busted plenty of horses back when I was working for other men. It ain't the right way. It takes the spunk out of them, or else it makes them mean and sneaky. Even old Buck there, it was a damn long time after he was made to using that he'd still turn loose of a sudden and try to bust back whoever was riding him, sometimes in some right inconvenient places. I don't ever mean to *bust* a Valdez horse."

He looked at the gray again. "I already done a damnsite more'n I should toward ruining that one. He ain't gonna forget that whip for a long time."

Back in the cabin, he got out a can of grease and set in to cleaning and oiling the saddle. He was working one-handed, letting his left arm rest on his leg and not moving much.

"I could do that," I suggested.

"I reckon you could," he agreed, but he didn't stop or show any sign of letting me.

"Don't your shoulder hurt?" I asked.

"No," he grunted, but I didn't believe him.

I cast around in my mind for another hint to throw at him. "It was a good thing I was here when that horse bit you. You needed somebody to bandage it up."

"Coulda done it myself," he mumbled, not looking up. "Was just easier to let you do it."

I set to thinking for some other argument why he should hire me on and I was deep into that thought when he did look up at me.

"You and the sheriff and that horse in ca-hoots again' me?" he said.

"Huh?"

"You're plumb determined you're gonna winter here, ain't you?"

"I'd like to," I owned.

"Can't afford to hire nobody," he mumbled. "And if I could, what makes you think I'd be hiring on some green kid what needs wet-nursing himself?"

"I ain't that green."

"Ain't you?" He rubbed hard at the saddle. For a long moment, he seemed intent on it. Then he said, "I can't pay you nothing. But if you want to hang around here till spring and hiring time on the ranches, and make yourself useful as you can, I'll feed you and I'll learn you about horses."

"Yes sir!" I pretty near jumped out of my chair. I didn't care all that much about the money. I needed a place to winter and I wanted to stay there with Chino a lot more than I wanted anything a few dollars could buy.

"All right," he sighed. He shoved the can of grease across the table toward me. "You'd better work on your own gear a bit. That kack of yours ain't much. The leather'll be cracking off it if you don't keep it right."

I fetched in my saddle and as I sat there working on it, I asked him, "What are you gonna do with the gray?"

He thought a moment before he answered me. "I got a notion maybe I'll trade him to the Arapahoe this winter. They're good with horses and what's between that gray and me is something personal. We just plain ain't never liked each other. Maybe he'd get on all right with the Indians."

"I heard Indians are awful hard on horses."

"I guess you've heard a damn lot of things about Indians," he muttered. "Well, they're just like everybody else. There's a mess of 'em and different ones got different ways. I've knowed white men were every bit as mean and hard on a horse as any Indian. Mostly the Indians understand horses better'n a white man. Lot of what I know about gentling, I learned off a tame Comanche." Picking up the quirt, he began to wash the dried blood off it.

"If you don't mean to be hard on the horses, why do you carry that whip?" I asked. It seemed like he had it hung off his wrist all the time.

He looked sidewise at me and drawled, "Well now, I ain't got hoofs and I don't reckon I could bite through a horse's hide if I was to be paid to do it."

"Huh?"

"There ain't anything ever yet jumped me that I couldn't back down with this here quirt," he explained.

I thought about it and asked him why he didn't carry a handgun if what he wanted was something to defend himself.

"It's awful easy to kill with a gun if you ain't careful," he said thoughtfully. "Man can make himself a mess of trouble that way."

He looked at me, his face kind of serious. But then he gave a flick of the quirt and grinned. "You ever watch a studhorse work his *manada?*"

I shook my head.

"He goes at them hoof and teeth. Sometimes he takes bloody chunks out their hides a lot worse'n that gray did mine. If I'm gonna boss horses, there's times I got to hurt them and more times I got to make them understand I *can* hurt them if I've got a mind to. With this lash I can just sting their hides or I can hurt 'em hard enough to drive off one when he takes a notion to stomp me the way that gray did."

79

I nodded that I followed what he was saying, and he added, " 'Sides, cartridges cost too damn much."

But it still seemed wrong to me that he didn't have a handgun. Most of the cowboys I'd seen on my travel had them and wore them on the range or into town. Like Mex boots and jangly spurs, a revolver was part of a cowboy's outfit that marked him as being a rider and not no ordinary man. Only Chino didn't wear high-heeled boots or spurs neither. And he sure wasn't from the common run of men.

He finished up working over his saddle and then poured water from the bucket into the basin. He flung his shirt and that rag into it to soak the blood loose.

"You any good at mending?" he asked me.

I shook my head.

"You can set into learning tomorrow," he said, keeping his face straight but looking amused around the eyes. "You want to work here — you can wash that out and when it's dry you can see what you can do about putting it back together."

That wasn't my idea of a riding man's job. I mumbled, "What for? It ain't worth the trouble."

"Ain't it?" he said. "Maybe that kack of yours ain't worth the bother, neither."

"Huh?" I looked at my old saddle. Maybe it wasn't much, but it was all I had.

"You ever get good and hungry or really cold, or you ever get your head set on something you really want, maybe you'll learn about making do with what you got," he muttered. "Right now, I reckon I'd better learn you how to patch up that old hull before it falls apart from under you one of these days. Got a knife?"

I dug out my Barlow knife and he fetched a piece of hide and showed me how to cut thongs. Then he went over the saddle with me, pointing out where the rigging was weakening and showing me how to mend it.

I had noticed the scars on his chest right after he'd stripped off his shirt but I'd been too concerned then with bandaging his shoulder to pay them any mind. But as we worked together on my saddle, I seen them again and I got curious about them. They were two small, ragged scars, almost just alike, one on either side through the fleshy part of his chest. I finally got up nerve enough to ask how he'd come by them.

"You ain't gonna believe me if I tell you," he said.

"I'll believe. I promise."

He looked at me sidewise. "That's a hell of a thing to say. How do you know what I'm gonna tell you? Only a damn-fool makes up his mind about a thing before he knows what it is."

I swallowed hard, feeling my face go red again. It seemed to me like I'd made a fool of myself more times since I'd met Chino than I had done in my whole life up to then. That was what come of being raised up in a house full of wimmen, I decided. If I'd had a father or big brothers to learn me right when I was young I'd have knowed better.

Chino got himself a cup of coffee and settled down, putting his heels on the table. Then he started talking.

"It was just after I left Texas. I come north the back way through some rough country and I kinda fell in with a bunch of Cheyenne. The way they invited me to stay a while at their camp, I couldn't exactly refuse, so I went along."

Remembering other stories I'd heard about wild Indians, I asked, "You mean they captured you?"

"Didn't nobody seem to know for sure. They treated me decent enough but they couldn't make up their minds was I company or a prisoner. I could make hand talk and their head man talked a little Spanish and we struck it off pretty good together. Some of the other chiefs objected though.

They said I wasn't nothing but just another white man and ought to be done with the same as all the rest.

"Well, one of the fellers pledged an *oxheheom* — what the whites call a sun dance. Him and some of his friends decided they'd fix my wagon good so they offered me a special invite to take part. They made it real clear I had my choice, figuring once I found out what I was supposed to do, I'd back out. Only I was real sure if I did back out the chief wasn't gonna call me *little brother* no more. And I figured what they wanted me to do wasn't gonna hurt any worse than getting my scalp took off would."

"What did they want you to do?" I asked

"You know what the sun dance is?"

"No."

"It's a big ceremony with a lot of parts to it, but the main thing is the dance. They put up a special lodge with a center pole that they hang ropes down from. The medicine man takes each feller that's gonna dance and he cuts a couple of little holes in his skin, here and here." He indicated the ends of each scar. "He pokes a sharp stick through each place and ties the end of one of those dangling ropes to it. You're supposed to dance till the skin tears loose.

Takes a hell of a lot longer'n you'd think, too."

I stared at the scars, swallowing hard to work up enough voice to ask him, "What happened then?"

"I done my part, not liking it much at all. And afterward I had this dream where the Maiyun — that's the Medicine Spirit — come to me. He told me I'd done all right and I was brother to the Cheyenne, but their life wasn't mine. He said I should pack up and get on to wherever I'd been going.

"I told the chief about it and he said I should do like the dream told me. He gave me a couple of horses and some Indian clothes and supplies and let me go. Told me I had honor in his camp and if I ever got tired of living white I should head on back and move in with him. There was times I thought of it, too. He was a right nice feller."

"Why didn't you?"

"Ain't no use. Times are changing. Too damn many white men. The Indians are losing their wars with 'em. The way the hunters are killing the buffalo, they'll all be gone before long too, and the blanket Indians can't go on living without them. Time's coming there ain't gonna be no wild Indians left." He swallowed what was left of his coffee, then added, "Nor wild Texicans neither. Man ain't got much choice but to settle down and learn to live white — if he wants to go on living."

I kept thinking about that story as I lay abed that night. It sounded sort of like some of the windies I'd heard on my travel. But the way Chino told it and the scars and all — I had a notion it wasn't any yarn. It seemed to me that if it was true of anybody, Chino'd be the one.

VI

The middle of the next day Buell Stanhope showed up. He drove his buckboard in and brought along that daughter of his. I found out he was in the habit off driving up regular until the snows came, bringing supplies and news and such. Chino didn't go to town often.

I stowed away the goods he brought and then went over to the corral where Chino was showing horses for Stanhope and his daughter. Seems she'd been living back East with an aunt or something for the past couple of years, going to school and learning all kinds of Eastern ways. Now that she'd come home again to stay Stanhope wanted to get her a saddle mount.

She was supposed to pick out one she liked and then Chino was to gentle it down proper for a lady. Only she didn't have any idea how to judge horseflesh and she just kept saying how pretty they were and what a cute little blaze this one had and what a darling way that one tossed its head and silly girl-things like that.

They messed around a time, having Chino show them one and another. Stanhope'd study on them and run his hands on their legs and frown. Chino would bring out each one Stanhope asked for. While he was standing, holding it for the inspection, he'd keep swinging that quirt against his leg. I got a notion Stanhope didn't have any idea what he was looking at in a horse either and that Chino was plumb disgusted with him.

But then the girl smiled and said, "Mister Valdez, I simply can't decide among them. They're all so nice. Would *you* pick one for me?"

Chino wheeled away from her and leaned his arm on the corral rail, resting his chin on it and looking at the horses. Even with his dark skin, I could see how red his face had gone and I think he'd turned away so that she wouldn't see too.

Real hearty and good-natured, like a drummer, Stanhope said, "What's the matter, Chino? Don't you have one that's good enough for my little girl here?"

That faded the high color right out of Chino's skin. I think for an instant he could have swung that whip into Stanhope's face. But he just straightened up and slapped it against his leg. Then he looked at the girl. He took a long, steady look at her and I will

87

admit that she wasn't hard to look at.

She was all done up in a suit of blue stuff that set off her soft yellow hair and shiny blue eyes. The ride up had made her cheeks all rosy and, looking at her, I begun to see for myself that women could be worth admiring now and then.

Real slow, Chino said, "I got a young mare out with the *manada* I'd figured on keeping with the herd. She'd likely make a good ladies' mount if I took her in hand."

"I'd like to see her," the girl told him.

He shifted his weight from foot to foot and looked at the ground as he answered, "I'll bring her up tomorrow. If Buell'll drive you over again in a couple of days, you can see her then."

"We can come, can't we, Father?" the girl said, taking hold of Stanhope's arm.

Chino added, "She's a pretty little filly. A white-stockinged sorrel with a blazed face. Got a fine little head and slim legs."

Legs is a word you ain't supposed to say in front of ladies. Stanhope's daughter blushed, turning her eyes down and pursing her lips in a funny little smile. Her dad stared real ornery at Chino.

He didn't seem to understand them at all. I suppose he hadn't run onto many Eastern-trained girls like that before.

Stanhope cleared his throat and said, "You bring the horse in. I'll bring Louise back to see it in about a week."

Chino nodded and Stanhope helped the girl up into the buckboard. Then he gestured for Chino to come into the cabin with him.

I followed along and inside Stanhope gave me a look that meant I was included in what he was saying. "I wish to hell you'd mind how you talk in front of Louise. She isn't one of the squaws you run with."

Chino switched the quirt against his leg, then pulled it off his wrist and hung it on a peg. Turning back to Stanhope, he said slow and hard, "What's the matter with the way I talk?"

"You got a mouth like a Texican," he answered. "My girl's been raised proper."

Chino's hands were clenched. He opened them slowly and looked past Stanhope at me. "You got any idea what he's talking about?"

I nodded, feeling my face flush a bit.

Holding his voice soft, Chino said, "All right, you can spell it out for me later."

As Stanhope stepped through the door, he called out, "Next time I come up, I'll bring you some drinking likker, Chino."

Chino wheeled and slammed his fist

against the wall. As he stood rubbing his knuckles, I could hear the buckboard rolling off. Real soft, under his breath, Chino muttered, "Some day I'm gonna cut out his gizzard and roast it slow."

Then he gave a shake of his head the same way you'll see a studhorse do. Like he couldn't understand it at all, he mumbled, "He sure threw a pretty filly there, though."

It was later that evening he mentioned her again. He had a mess of horse hair he'd spun up into yarn and he set down to show me how to braid a mecate for myself out of it. Once he got me started, he settled himself on his bunk with Banner curled up sleeping on the floor beside him. He just set, gazing off at nothing for a while. Then he said, "I think that sorrel filly's gonna be just the horse for that girl of Stanhope's. You reckon she knows anything about riding?"

"I dunno," I muttered. I had my doubts. She set me a lot in mind of my sister and I knew *she* wouldn't know which end of a bridle went over a horse's ears.

"Maybe she ought to come up here a few times," Chino said real soft. "I could give her some lessons. So's she wouldn't ruin the filly's mouth or get herself hurt or nothing like that."

I recalled then what Stanhope had said.

"If she does come, you gotta mind you don't say nothing about legs in front of her."

He looked sharp at me and asked, "What's wrong with legs? She's got 'em, ain't she?"

"I reckon. Only it just ain't a word you say in front of Eastern-trained ladies like her."

"Why not?"

I had to think on that. Best answer I could come up with was, "You just don't. It ain't considered proper. You don't use cuss words or talk about no parts of a body. You got to be awful careful what you say around ladies."

He snorted. "How the hell you gonna learn a lady how to ride if you can't tell her how to put her legs or that she's got her hands held wrong?"

"I guess you can say *hands* all right. It's the parts they cover up you can't talk about."

"Well, if I say a wrong thing, maybe she'll understand as how I don't mean nothing by it," he said. After a moment he added, "I got a mouth like a Texican."

I was sorry I'd brought it up. That crack of Stanhope's had rankled him deeper than I'd realized and now he was sulling over it. I decided I'd best not bother him with talk, not till he got over the mood he was in. I concentrated myself on making a neat job of braiding my hair rope and he just set with his own thoughts till it come time to bed down.

It was after he'd turned out the lamp and I was curled up under my buffalo robe, beginning to drowse, when he said real soft like he was talking to himself, "She sure is a handsome filly."

This time I knew he meant Stanhope's daughter and it bothered me the way he kept going back to her in his thoughts, though I couldn't have said why.

Chino wouldn't let me go along when he went to fetch up the sorrel filly. He said he wanted to bring her in without scaring her any more than he had to and he was afraid a stranger like me might spook the *manada*. So I stayed at the cabin to tend the chores and feed Banner.

Me and the foal both felt pretty lonely around there without him, but finally he come back with the filly. When I seen her, I knew what he'd meant about her being a ladies' horse. She was a perfect little lady herself, about thirteen-three, with a fine little muzzle and an arch to her neck and lithe legs. She was right excited and she pranced along, tossing her thick creamy mane and tail, and seeming like she barely touched her hoofs to the ground.

He turned her into the corral and came on inside to see if I had coffee on the stove. When he walked in Banner woke up and charged him like a puppy, climbing all over him. He started in to playing with the foal and told me if I wanted I could go out and see how friendly I could get with the filly, without I scared her.

I trotted off, feeling right excited about the idea. But I found out pretty quick that I couldn't get near to her. Every time I tried, she'd wheel and run off to the far side of the corral, pacing up and down the fence looking for a way out.

I talked soft and held out my hand and tried to sneak up real slow but it didn't do any good and finally I was beginning to tire myself out without ever laying a hand on her. Disappointed and disgusted with myself, I sat down on a fence rail and put my chin in my hands. I didn't want to go back inside and own to Chino as how I'd failed.

I was sitting there staring at the ground when I felt a warm breath on my cheek. I jerked up my head and the filly went dashing away. But she'd given me an idea, so I sat stock-still as I could.

It was awhile before she came back again,

but she finally did, high-lifting her hoofs and walking real wary with her eyes wide and her ears pointed. I could see her from the corner of my eye and I took care not to move my head. When she got closer I held my breath. She was real cautious, but she was as curious about me as she was scared of me.

Before long she got up close enough to start sniffing me over again. She breathed on my neck and down my collar. It tickled something awful but I held still. I figured I'd work my hand up slow and touch it to her neck. But I'd only just thought about it and not barely started to move when she reared and bolted again.

I let out my breath and caught another and we went through the whole business again. By the time she got to where she was nuzzling at me, the light was beginning to fade. But I was determined I'd put a hand on her before I quit. Only when I moved I spooked her again.

I was getting chilly sitting there and I could feel my nose needed wiping, but she was near me and I didn't want to scare her by moving. This time I already had my hand out where I wouldn't have far to reach to touch her.

She sniffed at my fingers and then stuck

out her tongue and licked my palm. I guess it had a salt taste to it. She gave it a big, slobbering lick and I slipped my fingers up and touched her under the chin.

She jerked up her head but she didn't bolt that time. With her head in the air, she seemed to be looking straight down her long nose at me. She gave a little snort, blowing right into my face. It reminded me how Chino had breathed up the foal's nostrils.

Real soft and easy, I blew my breath up her nose.

She stood as still as a statue, except for the twitching of her nostrils, and I reached out my hand, touching it to her chest. I didn't try to rub or scratch but just held my fingertips there. I felt her quiver her skin like she was trying to rid herself of a fly. And then with a snort, she bolted again.

But this time it wasn't me she'd run from, for I heard the cabin door open behind me and I was aware of lamplight spilling out of it. That was when I realized it was near dark and the night wind had come up real cold.

I dropped off the fence and headed to where Chino stood in the doorway. He stepped back as I walked in, and asked, "How'd you make out?"

"I breathed up her nose and put a hand on her chest," I said.

He looked at me curiously, with his head cocked. "Where'd you learn to breath up her nose?"

"I seen you do it with Banner," I answered, not sure from his tone whether I'd done right or wrong.

He grinned then and as he turned away, he muttered, "Maybe I'll make a *mesteñero* out of you yet."

"I done what I seen, but I don't know why," I told him.

"Quickest way you can get a horse to know you. A horse don't never *really* know you till you've shared breath with him."

The next day Chino started me to halter-breaking the filly, telling me what to do and watching me close while I done it. Before long, I had her to where she'd lead and she'd stand to have her hoofs handled and to be sacked out.

It was a couple of days later that Stanhope came back, bringing the load of canned milk Chino wanted. His daughter came with him to see the filly, but when she caught sight of Banner following along at Chino's heels, she just went wild with oohing and aahing over the foal.

At first it hid from her, behind of Chino's legs, peeking out around him. She thought that was cute. Pretty soon it got over being so shy and started sniffing her hand and then letting her scratch its head. And Chino got to talking to her about the little feller.

She was asking all sorts of questions and in the beginning he just gave her short stiff answers without quite meeting her eyes. But before long he got to talking as free with her as he did with me, telling her all about Banner and the clever things he did. I don't think Chino could have cared much more for a kid of his own than he did for that foal. And it showed so much in his face I reckon the girl could see it too.

She kept smiling at the foal and carrying on over it the way females do over baby things. Then she got to smiling at Chino sort of the same way. But he was so much involved in talking about Banner and the *manada* that he didn't seem to notice.

It was Stanhope interrupted them, saying as how they'd come to look at the filly and they couldn't stay long on account of it got dark so early that time of year. Then Chino sent me in to fetch her and show how I could handle her.

She was kind of nervous about so many people but she calmed down for me. The girl wanted to mess around with her. Chino had to explain she wasn't really tamed yet. He suggested they come visit again in a week or so and he'd have her shaped up by then.

The girl asked her father could she come and he sort of agreed, though he wasn't any too eager about it himself. I could tell there was still bad feeling between him and Chino.

The girl had to pet Banner some more before she was willing to leave, and when Stanhope finally got her back into the buckboard, she waved goodbye and Chino waved back at her.

Then he walked off upslope a ways with Banner at his heels and settled himself on an outcrop of rock. He just sat there a long while, gazing out over the ranch but seeming like he wasn't really looking at anything in particular. It was twilight before he came down again.

VII

Chino started working the filly himself. He explained to me how he had to get her well along before Miss Stanhope came back to see her again. After I'd watched him work awhile I understood as how what he could do in a few hours would have taken me days.

My chores were pretty light and Chino was too busy with the horses to set me more tasks or learn me anything much so I spent a fair bit of time riding Buck and the rest of it sitting on the fence rails just watching Chino. I guess maybe I was learning from that because I begun to get ideas of what he was doing and why.

Sometimes after supper I'd try to get him to talk to me about the work. He was willing enough but he'd stretch out on his bunk and before I could get more than a couple of questions out, he'd be asleep. So I had to do my learning on my own, trying to figure out the reasons he handled the horses the way he did.

Watching him that way, I seen other things too. I seen how when something would go wrong or a horse would fight back at him or just learn too slow to suit him, he had a way of hesitating and slapping the quirt against his leg. When I studied on it, I began to understand that this slow, easy, patient manner wasn't any more natural to Chino than working under a saddle is to a horse. It was something he'd had to learn and all the time he was working with the horses, he was tight-reining himself. When a thing went against him, I think his natural way would have been to strike out at it, the way he'd done with that whip when the gray bit him.

He didn't though. He'd just hesitate and then go back at whatever he was working at, as gentle and patient with the horses as spring sunshine. When he flicked one with the quirt there was always a reason I could see and understand if I thought on it.

Stanhope and his daughter hadn't yet come back when the first snow fell. There'd been several days of drizzle and then this sprinkling of snow. I guess it made the road up pretty rough traveling.

That same day a few horses of the herd drifted into sight down the park. Chino'd told me they'd show up, come snowfall. They always ranged downvalley in the spring, traveling a long ways into the deep lush grass. But when winter was coming on, they'd head back. When the snow got so bad that there wasn't enough graze he'd start sledding hay down from the barn for them.

Well, snow came as a real surprise to Banner. When Chino started out that morning, it wasn't falling any more, but there was a fair cover of it on the ground. Banner set out behind of Chino as usual. He frisked up to the door, not paying much mind to where he was going and he set foot right in the snow without seeing it. At that he went up onto his hind legs like a snake had bit him, his eyes all wide and shocked. When he came down again with his forehoofs inside the threshold, he poked his nose down and started studying over the snow.

Chino and I both stopped to watch. The foal smelled over every inch as far as his baby neck would reach, snuffling and snorting and grunting with disgust. Then he took a long look at Chino like it was all his fault and a real mean trick.

Chino just grinned and started walking away, watching over his shoulder. Banner didn't like that either. He raised up his head and called his pitiful sad little nicker.

"Come on," Chino said to him.

He danced a bit there inside the door, fretting and worrying. But he seen Chino wasn't coming back no matter how hard he begged so he tried putting a hoof down onto the snow. He looked like he figured it would break through and drop him straight to hell.

When he found out there was firm ground under the first hoof, he tried another, every bit as cautious. Before long he got all four onto the snow and then took a step, sniffing and studying the ground first, picking out a place to set his hoof. He lifted it up high as he could and brought it down easy.

After a few steps he decided it was all right and trotted off after Chino with his head up and his stub of a tail flagged out. A few minutes more and he was tearing around showing off how much snow he could kick up at each stride. Then he tried rolling in it and when he got up he shook himself like a dog to get it all off his long baby fuzz.

It started snowing again that night and this time it got right serious about it. For almost a week it came down frequent, until it was fair deep in the hollows, and the horses down the valley kept moving closer to the cabin.

Chino was unhappy about all that snow. He told me Stanhope had already brought all the winter supplies and likely he and his daughter wouldn't be coming back now that the road was snowed over. But he kept glancing off that way like he hoped to catch sight of them.

I noticed he got to keeping watch toward the sky downvalley too. One day I seen him gazing off that way, squinting against the brightness of the sun on the snow, like he seen whatever he was looking for. I went over and asked him what it was.

"Yonder," he said with a grin. "You see smoke against the sky over there?"

I looked hard as I could but I didn't see it.

"That's Walks-Away's people," he told me. "They've made their winter camp."

"Who's Walks Away?" I asked, still trying to spot the smoke.

"Friend of mine," he said. "He's chief of a band of Arapahoe the troopers ain't quite tamed yet. His whole name comes out something on the order of *When the People Gather and the Chiefs Meet to Talk Things Over He Gets Into Arguments and Walks Away.* Only that ain't easy for a white man to say in Arapahoe so we call him Walks-Away for short."

"You know him?"

"Sure. I reckon you and me ought to ride over and say hello while the ridges are still clear."

That got me pretty excited and I wanted to leave then and there. I'd seen some tamed blanket Indians on my travel, but never no wild ones. The notion of going to visit their camp — well, that was the kind of thing I'd been dreaming about doing when I left for the West.

Chino only laughed and told me we had work to finish at the ranch before we went packing off on social calls. But that didn't cool me down any and finally he promised we'd set out in a couple of days if the weather held good.

It held and at last Chino turned out all but some using horses and that evening he started packing for the trip. He told me we'd be traveling along the high trails to avoid the drifts, so we'd be most of a day going each way. We could stay a night at the Indian camp, but that was all, on account of the work we had at the ranch. But from the amount of stuff he was packing it looked like he meant to be gone for a week or two. He went through the stock of goods Stanhope had brought in, picking out airtights of peaches, a good-sized bag of tobacco, a jug of sweet'ning, coffee and stuff like that. I commented how it seemed like an awful lot, but he just said, "Not for a trip to see Walks-Away."

Then he got to telling me how the Indians came every winter to camp on one of the sheltered slopes down at the end of the valley and live off the game that came down looking for graze when the high slopes froze over. They were fair friendly Indians, he said, though they didn't care much for having to do with white men. That made me feel a little doubtful about our going to visit, but Chino said they didn't exactly count him as a white man and he reckoned they wouldn't mind him bringing a friend, long as I behaved myself.

The next morning he put a packsaddle on Buck and caught a sandy bay for himself. While I was saddling up my mare, he neck-roped that mean gray and a lineback dun for easy herding. Then we set out with Banner trailing along.

I was eager as all get-out and anxious to hurry, but he kept to an easy pace and all the while he'd point out things to me along the way. I guess there must have been millions of things for a greenhorn like me to see. He showed me tracks in the snow and told me about the animals that made them and things like that. And he kept telling me to look-see game off in the woods, though I never spotted half what he said was there.

Well, we finally come onto the Arapahoe camp. It was maybe a dozen or so tipis set in a circle down in a sheltered park. Grazing off from the tipis were at least as many horses as in Chino's cavvy, and they sure were a mixed lot — all different sizes, though mostly small, and every different color that horses come in.

The people I seen inside the circle of tipis were mostly women and kids. The women were working at things like stretching and scraping hides and sewing. And the kids were all ducking behind of tipis and shield posts and drying racks to stare at us as we rode in.

We got met first by a mess of dogs that raced around yapping at us. Then a few old men bunched together and walked over. One of them lobbed some stones at the dogs and drove them away before they started in to chewing at our horses. Him and Chino exchanged a few words, with the old man doing most of the talking. It was all in their language, excepting a few American words. Most of them were words I was still inclined to blush at, but they seemed to be a right important part of Indian talk. I noticed Chino hesitated a lot like he didn't speak their language too good, but they done a fair bit of hand-gesturing and he was real good at that.

They seemed pleased to see us and after a minute Chino told me to step down and take the horses off into the grass, but not to tether them too close to the Indian herd. I went upvalley a ways with them and when I got back all the kids and dogs were running around the camp like must have been normal for them. Chino was nowhere to be seen.

I didn't know what to do and I didn't think I ought to start hollering for him like I was a lost calf, though I felt a bit that way. I just stood there, sort of peeking out from between a drying rack and a tipi, coming to the opinion that I wasn't none too comfortable by my lonesome among all them Indians, even if they were all women and kids. I told myself Chino wouldn't have left me alone if it wasn't safe for me, but I was having trouble convincing my spine of it.

Just then a couple of boys about half my age came tearing past me, each one slapping at me and giving out a whoop. I jumped. Without thinking, I wheeled and slapped at the trailing one same as if I was still a kid and had been tagged by some other boy without expecting it. Minute I hit him, I realized what I was doing and it scared me stiff.

It gave the Indian kid a start too. He wheeled and stared at me for a moment. Then he gave out another whoop and charged toward me. I seen it was all a game and I hadn't done wrong hitting him, so I made a grab to tag him again. But he swerved and got away from me.

Next thing I knew I was mixed up with a whole bunch of them, all of us running and dodging and trying to tag each other. I got to hollering same as them and jumping around till I was beginning to sweat. They was sure fast of foot.

I was just diving to tag a little feller who was ducking under the drying rack when something caught me by the back of the collar. Real sudden I recollected that it was wild Indians I was among, and I froze up.

Then I heard Chino's voice. "Hold on there, before you get your scalp lifted."

I squirmed around to see it was him had hold of me. He grinned and I seen he was kidding. He asked me, "What the hell you up to?"

I told him how I come to be playing with the Indian kids and he explained to me they'd been making out I was an enemy and when they slapped me they'd been counting coup on me. If I tagged one of them, I counted coup back. It seems like I'd got myself into an Indian war without I even knew it.

By then all the kids were hiding behind things again, looking wide-eyed at us and listening to everything Chino said, though they couldn't a one of them have understood a word of American. I asked Chino were they afraid of him.

He grinned again and said, "Kinda. I got spirit friends. I make strong medicine."

But before I could ask him what he meant, I heard a real whoop from off to the ridges. I jerked around and seen a whole row of riders lined up on top the ridge we'd rode over. They were growed men and all armed. My first thought was they were Indian enemies of the Arapahoe and they were about to swoop down and attack the camp and slaughter all of us.

Before I could swallow my heart down out my throat, Chino had given a whoop back and set out at a run. He flung off his hat and peeled his coat, dropping it as he ran. Stopping with his feet apart, out in the clear beyond the tipis, he threw back his head and gave another holler.

I'd started after him with no idea what was happening, but good and scared. Only one of the old Indian men stopped me. I stood there feeling his hands like claws gripping my arms and watching.

An Indian in that line of riders moved his horse forward a step. He handed his rifle and robe to the man next to him and stretched out his arms. Then he charged.

The horse he sat was a fair big blue roan

and it come down the slope with a snorting and pounding of hoofs like a locomotive. Chino stood his ground and I thought for sure the horse was gonna run right over him. But just as it was almost on top of him, it swerved. The Indian leaned way over, grabbing at Chino and Chino grabbed at him.

Next thing I knew, they were both on the ground, rolling over and over together. It looked like they meant to kill each other. I pulled loose of the old man's hands and ran toward them. There wasn't anybody gonna kill Chino if I could help it.

I don't know what I figured to do, seeing I wasn't armed except for the Barlow knife in my pocket. And I didn't even think about that right then. All I could think was that buck meant to kill Chino.

But I stopped myself short when I seen what they were doing was wrassling.

It didn't last long. Suddenly the Indian was astride of Chino's chest, knees pinning his arms, and he had a hand wrapped into his hair. Chino bucked and struggled, but the Indian was a fair bit bigger'n him and as broad as a barn. For all his twisting, Chino couldn't break loose. When he gave up and lay still the Indian raised both hands to show everybody watching and gave another holler. Then he leaped to his feet.

Chino jumped too. The Indian tried to catch him with a slap, same as those kids had caught me, but Chino was too fast afoot for him and slapped him instead. Then they threw their arms over each other's shoulders and tromped toward the camp, laughing fit to bust.

The rest of the men rode down from the ridge then, whooping and hollering and doing some right fancy riding. I found out they were the men of the camp and had been out hunting when we got there.

I trotted toward Chino. By then I was getting over being scared and was starting to feel disappointed at how easy he'd been licked in the wrassling match.

"He *beat* you!" I said.

Chino laughed. "Sure, he scalps me every time he meets me when I'm afoot. But he ain't been able to unhorse me yet. And I get him off his horse every time. 'Sides, I counted coup on him."

Then he introduced me, saying a few words in Arapahoe to the Indian. He told me, "This here is Walks-Away's oldest boy. His name is sort of *He Wrassles with Everybody He Meets and Licks 'em All.* The Wrassler for short."

The Wrassler took hold of my hand and pumped it a bit. Then some more Indians come up and Chino introduced me to the rest of them, Walks-Away among them. Each one worked my hand a while, and Chino explained to me they'd learned this off the white men.

We all went into one of the tipis and I was right surprised by it. It was a lot bigger inside than I'd expected. There was a wall of hides hung down from the poles and tucked under the robes of the floor so that there wasn't any draft. With the fire going in the middle, it was a lot snugger inside than our cabin.

There was furnishings, too. Little beds that sat a ways up off the floor and had backrests to them, and robes, and the kind of leather bags white men call parfleches, and cooking and eating tools. It was real pleasant and homey.

We all sat around the fire and I begun to get drowsy as Chino and the Indians smoked and talked together. He made presents to them of all those extra supplies we'd brought and they gave him pelts and a parfleche of pemmican and dried meat. Then they got to talking about the horses Chino'd brought to trade. I guess I dozed off, 'cause next thing I knew Chino and I were alone, excepting for an Indian girl who'd been working away in the back of the tipi. She come over and talked to Chino a bit. Then he seen I was awake and he introduced me to her.

She was Walks-Away's daughter, *Fast and Light of Foot as the Antelope.* What he called her for short was some Mex word that I heard him say a few times. But he never told it to me.

She was round-faced with high-set cheekbones and she looked odd to me till I got used to Indian looks. Then I decided she was fair handsome. She wore a long-fringed buckskin dress that was like a big sack with sleeves. It only came down to around her knees, but her legs were all wrapped with furs so I reckon it was respectable enough. She had a lot of beads and things around her neck. Among them was a big Mex silver belt buckle hung on a thong. I noticed how she'd drop her eyes to it and smile soft as she fingered at it. Later I found out Chino had given it to her.

Well, him and her talked to each other a bit and then he told me to go on outside and amuse myself.

I went, feeling kind of lonely. It bothered me, the way he'd just up and sent me off. For a while I wandered around. Then I begun to get interested in the things that was going on in the camp.

'Specially I got interested in watching one girl making moccasins. She was stitching on those little trade beads into patterns and they were about as nice a pair of moccasins as the ones Chino wore.

I watched for a while, admiring them and wishing I had me a pair. I thought about trying to buy them off her, but I didn't have a cent to my name, nor anything to offer in trade. Then I remembered my Barlow knife. It was a pretty nice one and I was right proud of it. But I surely did want a pair of moccasins like Chino had.

I pulled out the knife and showed it to her, telling her I wanted to swap, though she didn't understand a word I said. I tried gesturing and pointing. She frowned a bit as she watched my hands. Then she looked down at the ground, real shy, and she took my knife. Only she didn't give me the moccasins. She grabbed them in one hand and my knife in the other and run off into a tipi.

I figured she must have thought I was making her a present of the knife, but I didn't know how to explain different. And I didn't think I'd better go into that tipi after her. So I stuck my hands in my pockets and walked off, kicking at rocks and feeling pretty low. Now I didn't even have my knife and if there's anything a man on the frontier needs as much as a horse, it's a knife.

I decided I'd tell Chino and maybe he could explain to the girl. But I didn't see him again till he called me to come eat. And then he was so much involved with talking to the Indians and I felt so left out that I didn't mention it at all. He wasn't paying me any mind and I got to feeling so awful alone that soon as I could I excused myself and went outside.

The moon was up and near full, and the air was crisp but not too cold on account we were so well sheltered from the wind. I went off and hung around with our horses for awhile, scratching my mare under the chin and talking out loud to her. But she went to sleep on me.

When I got back to camp everything was real quiet and I still felt strange and lonesome about the way Chino'd been treating me. I wasn't sure what I ought to do about sleeping. I supposed he was bedded down with Walks-Away's family and I guessed if I had stayed put in the tipi I would be too. But I didn't feel like sneaking in to find out so I got my bedroll from under the tarp we'd wrapped the saddles in. I legged it off a ways and found me a sheltered place between some rocks and a big log where the pine needles were deep and soft. I spread my blankets there and settled down.

It was chilly lying out, but it seemed to fit with the chilly feeling I had inside. I just lay there being miserable and after a while I begun to drowse off. I come awake though at the touch of a hand on my shoulder. My thought was it was Chino come looking for me. But then I seen it wasn't him at all. It was that girl who'd took my knife.

She dropped down to her knees and said something soft to me as she touched my face with her fingertips. It gave me a feeling I hadn't ever had before. I was awful young and awful green then and I didn't know what was happening. But after a while I begun to get the idea.

VIII

When the dawn wakened me, the girl was gone. And I didn't even know her name.

I laid there wrapped in my blankets and thinking over what had happened. I don't reckon I was ever any more confused in my life. By everything I'd ever been learned I was sure what I'd done was awful wrong. But yet it was wonderful and she was a wonderful girl and I — well, I was damn sure then that I was a growed man.

I finally got up and rolled my blankets. It was kind of late when I walked back into the camp. I found Chino outside Walks-Away's tipi, gnawing on a meat bone and talking with a couple of bucks. He shot me a funny look that gave me the sudden horrible feeling that he knew all about what had happened that night. I felt my face go burning red and wheeled to get away from him quick as I could.

But he called after me, "Hold on there. You want to eat before we leave?"

I guess I was hungry enough, but I sure didn't feel like eating. I just shook my head.

Chino'd already saddled up. He took his leave of the Indians and we rode off. He didn't talk none and neither did I. I was busy trying to straighten out my thoughts and not having any luck at it. I was awful mixed up about being proud of the man I was and happy over what I knew now but yet I knew I'd done wrong and I felt shamed by it.

I had a notion Chino knew what I'd done and I wondered was he mad at me for it. I felt cut off from him and real alone. Miserable as I was about that, I couldn't think of no way to get friendly with him again.

We'd been riding a long while when he reined up and asked me was I hungry yet. I nodded but I didn't say anything. I couldn't meet his eyes.

He stepped down and opened one of the parfleches on the packsaddle. He slabbed off a chunk of the dried meat the Indians had gave us and I set in to chewing on it.

After he'd cut himself a chunk, he dug into the other parfleche. What he brought out this time was a pair of moccasins. He held them toward me and I seen they were the ones that girl had been making. My face must have flamed up like coal-oil on a fire. I was so ashamed of myself I could hardly make my hand move to take them.

Chino turned his back to me as he started closing the parfleche again. Kind of gruff, he said, "Well, you come out to this part of the country to learn growing up, didn't you?"

I nodded, though he couldn't see it with his back turned.

"You're learning, ain't you?" he said, like he knew what I'd answered.

I gave another little nod.

"Then what the hell you worrying about?" He jerked at the packsaddle cinches and then looked up at me. He was grinning.

Everything was all right! He wasn't mad at me and he wasn't shamed by me. What I'd done — well, it couldn't have been *too* wrong.

I grinned back, feeling my face still burning.

When we moved out, he set into talking to me and we were together again, the way we'd been before. He didn't say anything about that girl or the moccasins but he got to telling me about Indian ways. It reminded me how he'd said he made strong medicine and I asked him what he'd meant by that.

"First winter I had the *manada* in the valley I didn't yet have the cabin built and I was lying out, close to the herd," he begun. "Some of the young bucks from Walks-

119

Away's camp seen how it was and that was more temptation than they could stand. Thieving, especially horse-thieving, ain't wrong by their lights, you know. They honor a good horse thief for his skill. And those bucks felt like they just had to take some of the mares out from under my nose. They did too, and I got pretty mad about it."

"What did you do?"

"I stole 'em back. I ain't a bad horse thief myself. But that only got them more interested. They stole 'em again and I stole 'em back again. Third time, I seen where it was getting to be a game with them. It was one I didn't have the time or notion to play. I thought on riding down to their camp and holding a one-man massacre but I seen if I did, I'd likely be the man who got massacreed. I decided again' that, so I picked a couple of mares to take as gifts and I painted hands on Buck's rump to show I wasn't a nobody-white man but had took a scalp or two myself . . ."

"Had you?"

He nodded and went on ". . . and I peeled my shirt to show my scars. Then I rode down into their camp. They didn't much like the idea of a white man riding in that way, but I got them curious enough they accepted my presents and palavered with me.

"I didn't have no Arapahoe words then but I had a few Cheyenne, which Walks-Away can talk. And I had plenty-enough sign talk to make myself understood. I told Walks-Away and Medicine Horn — the old medicine man, he died last year — what I was trying to do building the ranch and how I didn't have time to play games with his bucks and wouldn't put up with having my herd raided."

He paused so I hurried him on by asking what had happened then.

"He asked me what I was gonna do about it. I had some fool notion I could bluff my way through, so I said I'd make strong medicine against his people if they didn't leave me be. I didn't know nothing about the Arapahoe spirits but I told them I was brother to the Cheyenne and favored by the Mayiun. They listened me out and then asked me to prove it.

"That was when I got to worrying a bit. It didn't look like they were gonna bluff easy and I'd never made medicine in my life. I'd knowed Comanches and Apaches down south, as well as the Cheyenne, and I'd seen some of the things they done. But I knowed, too, what could happen to a white man what got Indians mad at him. And I had a notion if they figured out I was bluffing I wasn't gonna leave that camp very happy."

In a small voice, I asked him, "What did you do?"

"I made strong medicine."

"Huh?"

"You can laugh if you want," he said. "Only I didn't see any other way out of what I'd got myself into. I recollected how the Mayiun come to me in my dream and, seeing as how I'd danced for him, I was hoping maybe he'd remember me. I didn't rightly know how to call on him. But I hoped he'd have pity on a damnfool veho like me so I set in best I could. Walks-Away and Medicine Horn were real willing to give me every chance to prove myself, so Medicine Horn burned some stuff and chanted for me."

As he described it I could see them in my mind — him and the two Indians sitting at the fire inside of a half-dark tipi, with the smoke rising and the firelight flickering on the walls and the wind blowing through the lodgepoles. The air had been thick with the scents of the burning herbs, and smoke from their pipes. Medicine Horn had leaned back his head, rocking as he chanted. Then Chino'd begun to talk, hoping the Mayiun would hear him.

"I knew he'd understand American 'cause that was how he'd talked to me in my dream," he told me, "so I set in to explaining my troubles to him, telling him how I'd worked and planned so damn long to get the ranch started and how I'd put in better'n two years of working to pay the price for Flag and then gone pardners with that bastard, Stanhope. Now I was finally on the way toward getting what I wanted but if the Arapahoe didn't let me be, I'd lose it all."

His voice dropped down as he talked and I could imagine how he'd been speaking to the Mayiun in that same soft-voiced chanting way that he coaxed the horses when he worked them. "Medicine Horn begun to nod his head while I was saying my piece and I wasn't sure whether he was agreeing with me or just falling asleep. But I kept telling the Mayiun how it was and wondering if he heard me at all and if he'd favor me or just figure I was a damnfool for bothering him with my troubles. I was beginning to really worry that he wouldn't pay me no mind when suddenly Medicine Horn let out a holler. I guess I near to jumped out of my skin.

"Well, Medicine Horn set into laying out some long story for Walks-Away. When he was done, Walks-Away explained it to me.

Medicine Horn had said that while I was talking the Horse-Spirit come to him. The Horse-Spirit had said as how I was telling the truth and he wanted me raising my horses to honor him. He'd said the Arapahoe should leave me be so's I could do the work that was mine to do.

"Afterward, Walks-Away promised to make his bucks let me be. He said I was welcome in his lands and to show it was so, he gave me two real fine brood mares and told me I should come visit his camp again. He come down to visit me a few times, too, and even brought me meat when he'd had a good hunt, on account he knew I didn't have much time to hunt for myself. He's a real fine feller, Walks-Away. 'Bout the best friend I got. Treats me like one of the family."

After we got back to the cabin and I'd bedded down for the night, I lay a while thinking over everything that had happened at the Arapahoe camp and the things Chino'd told me. I kept remembering that girl who'd made the moccasins. Then I recalled Walks-Away's daughter and how she'd worn Chino's buckle on a thong around her neck and how she'd smiled at him and him back at her. I guessed I understood then why he'd left me alone so much of the time. I didn't really blame him for it.

Time passed quick. Chino didn't seem to pay much attention to such things, but I kept track of the days. And all of a sudden I realized it was coming on toward Christmas. I asked him about that and whether he done something special to celebrate. He looked a little surprised at the idea and asked me was it an important day to me.

I told him how it was about the most important holiday there is. He said it was that way with the Mexicans, too, and asked me how my people celebrated.

I said we kept the old country custom of having a Christmas tree and I got to telling him all about how back home we'd decorate the house with green stuff and bring in a little pine tree and put do-pretties all over it and have a big dinner and go calling on folks and give presents and all. But when I asked him back what they did where he came from, all he said was that they didn't have trees enough to waste on things like that down there.

I decided he must not be in the habit of paying Christmas any mind and I figured if that was his way it was good enough for me. But still I had a strong feeling I'd like to give him a present. Only I didn't have any money to buy one with and I didn't have any notion of anything I could make that would be a fitting present for him.

He rode out that afternoon and it wasn't till after dark that he got back. I was inside then, starting supper, and when he came in he had this little spruce sapling over his shoulder. He stood it up and gave it a turn, looking at it real critical.

Kind of gruff, he said, "There's your tree. You can do what you want with it."

I decided then that no matter what, I *had* to give him a present of some kind. After supper, while I made a stand to hold up the tree I was still thinking on it. The tree was a nice-shaped little one, not quite as tall as me but well filled-out. I got it stood up in the corner and then started looking for things to decorate it with.

Back home we'd used fruits and berries strung on thread, candles and store-bought geegaws. Chino didn't have anything like that around the place but I scrounged up some air-tights we'd emptied but not yet buried. I hacked them into pieces, poked holes in them and tied them onto the branches. They turned a bit in the drafts and flashed the lamplight real pretty.

It needed some color though and I mentioned it. Chino frowned, studying over the tree, and then he dug into the chest. He come up with a bright red neckerchief that had a fair-sized hole in it. We tore that and some of the muslin sheeting into strips and hung them on. And we made some little geegaws out of bits of different-colored horsehair he'd been saving. When we were done it was a long ways from the kind of fancied-up tree we'd had back in Savannah, but it sure looked nice to me.

I lay awake a long while that night, thinking on what I could give him for Christmas. Finally I determined if I worked real hard at it, I could finish up my mecate and make him a present of that. It sure wasn't much and it really wasn't even mine on account of it was him who'd saved the hair and spun the yarn. But he'd said the mecate would be mine when I finished it. And it was the only thing I had that I could figure him having any use for at all.

A couple of days later, when we had finished supper and settled in for the evening, he suddenly asked me, "You want to go into town tomorrow?"

"Huh?" I was working hard at the mecate and only half-heard what he'd said.

"I got to run an errand in town. Thought you might like to go along," he told me. "There's big doings — dancing and partying and such. Christmas celebrating. I've heard tell near the whole county turns out for it. Never been myself, but I get a mite curious sometimes."

I understood what he meant was he was offering to take me in for the party. I got all excited at the idea.

He grinned at me and said, "All right. We'd better bed early 'cause there's a lot to be done in the morning before we leave."

Well, I curled up under my buffalo robe but I couldn't fall asleep for a long while, what with thinking about the party. Until he'd suggested it, I hadn't had a thought about going to town. But now I was every bit as excited as a little kid.

I got to wondering would he let me ride the sorrel geld down. It would be real fine to ride into town with my spurs polished and a fine piece of horseflesh between my knees. The sorrel would be tossing its head, rattling the bit and showing what a real horse he was. And I'd be sitting him the way Chino'd learned me, like a *mesteñero.*

Then I got to worrying over whether I should wear the high-heeled boots with the spurs on them, cowboy-fashion, or the moccasins the Indian girl had given me. There surely wouldn't be many folks had on real Indian moccasins like that. Anybody who had the money could buy himself a pair of boots, but when a feller had a pair of moccasins that had been given to him by a wild blanket Indian girl after he'd visited at the camp and he'd — he'd — well, a feller wearing moccasins like that, there couldn't nobody call *him* just a green kid, could they?

We both hurried through our chores the next morning. Then we slicked up and I had just about decided to wear my moccasins when I seen Chino dig into the chest and come up with a pair of high-heeled Mex boots that had about the biggest spurs I ever seen on them. He put them on and when he walked the rowels tapped the ground at each step. They rang like bells.

I could see the boots had been worn a lot and I asked him why he didn't wear them now when he worked the horses. He'd already showed me how to use my own spurs to signal a horse and he'd explained that spurs weren't just for raking holes in a mean horse and impressing the girls, like so many cowboys seemed to think. They could be used real handy without they hurt the horse at all.

"Back when I busted horses fast and hard I used to wear them," he answered me. "But I've kinda got out of the habit." Then he muttered, "I wouldn't want to rake up no

129

Valdez horse and be sorry for it later."

Well, when he finished getting dressed up, I was right surprised by him. He had a shirt that was hardly faded at all and over it a black leather vest with conchos that looked like real silver. He brushed his britches near clean and tucked them into those boots. He'd scrubbed good and shaved real close for a change. With that sash around his waist and his hat set square on his head, he looked about as flash as any cowboy I'd seen — excepting he didn't wear a gun.

He'd given me a piece of rattlesnake skin to make a band for my hat and I had a bright red bandanna at my throat. With my spurs all polished and that sorrel horse under me I felt right slick myself when we left out for town.

IX

It was already twilight when we got to Jubilee, but there were lamps lit all along the main street, giving a warm friendly glow to everything. A fair lot of people were in town and most of 'em seemed to be standing around the plank walks. I'm sure there wasn't many of them knew us, but they'd holler out greetings anyway, and Chino'd grin and holler back. I did too.

That sorrel horse under my saddle hadn't ever been to town before and he was raising a ruckus, tossing his head so his mane flagged out and dancing his hoofs, sidestepping and twisting against the bit. I had my hands full with him, but I could hear the rattle of the bit and the jingle of my spurs and I sat tall and straight. I don't guess there was anybody ever felt any prouder than I did then.

Chino drew rein in front of Langer's Mercantile and told me to mind the horses while he tended his errand. I did, sitting there and easing my feet out the stirrups. I let my legs hang, the way he did so much, despite the way that sorrel was carrying on. I guess luck was with me on account I was still on its back when Chino came out of the store. He had a little package wrapped in brown paper and he stuffed it into his saddlebag, then mounted up and we rode on.

The place the party was to be was a ways off the main street and as we headed toward it, Chino spoke to me, his voice soft and serious. "Boy, don't let me get started in to drinking tonight."

"Huh?"

"You see me set in on the hard likker, you stop me."

I knew a lot of fellers went strong for drinking likker, especially at celebrations and I'd been thinking of trying it myself now that I was a growed man. I didn't understand why Chino'd said what he did. I said, "It's a party."

"Yeah," he muttered. "Only I can't no more handle firewater than a redskin. You see me, you stop me."

I agreed I would, but then we caught sight of the barn and I didn't think no more of what he'd said.

It wasn't a plain old feed-and-stock barn but a big wood-floored wagon shed that the freight line used for storage in the winter months. Come Christmastime every year the wagons were hauled out and used to make a sort of ring around the front of the building for a windbreak and a barbecue was set up there.

We could smell the meat cooking before we got to the barn and it set me to thinking how long it had been since breakfast. When we'd picketed our horses, we walked over to the firepits and I seen there were already a lot of folks there.

Cold as it was on the slopes, the fires filled up that little circle inside the wagons with warmth and the fellers doing the cooking were stripped to their shirt-sleeves.

Nothing over the fire was near done enough for eating yet but there was a table spread with all kinds of other good foods like pies and cakes and salads and things that the women had made up special for the party. When I found out all them eats was there for a man to help himself I lit in. By the time I'd got the edge took off my appetite, I'd lost track of Chino. I heard the music swelling out of the barn and I decided to look in there.

It was a big place all decorated with branches and paper streamers and tinsel do-pretties. There were enough lanterns hung off the rafters to make it almost bright as day.

I slid on in with the folks who were lined up against the walls watching the dancing. The music was real good foot-stomping stuff. And the folks in the squares were decked out in their fancy clothes. It was fun to watch and I stood awhile, enjoying it all. Then the music stopped and they started making up new squares. Next thing I knew, I was into one of them.

Well, I got to swinging and stepping and really enjoying myself. And when we did some partner-changing figures I got matched with a girl about my own age who set me in mind of that Arapahoe girl. I don't mean she looked like an Indian because she didn't. She was light-complected with yellow hair and a little button of a nose all covered with freckles and she had on frilly gingham. But still somehow she reminded me of the Indian girl — only she wasn't near so shy. Her eyes were blue and bold and laughing. And she looked at me so straight on that I busted right out and asked her would she be my partner in the next set.

She said yes.

Her name was Annie Johnson and she wasn't anything like my sister and all those silly, giggly girls back East. That night, dancing with her, I reckoned she wasn't like anybody else in the whole world. She was light and graceful of foot as that sorrel filly back to the ranch. When I danced with her I felt like I was flying. I hadn't never danced as well or had as much fun doing it as I did with her. When the next set made up, I wanted to keep right on going. But she begged off that she was out of breath and suggested we walk outside together to get a bite of cake.

Though I felt shy of doing it, I took her arm as we went out. Recalling the Eastern manners I'd put out of my mind on my travel, I cut a piece of the cake for her and got her a cup of the fruit punch. She seemed real pleased by it.

I knew I was blushing and hoped it wouldn't show by the firelight and I tried hard to keep from stammering when I talked with her. But my tongue kept tripping over itself.

She didn't make fun of me for it though. And when she talked, she was so straightforward, not being coy or cute, but meeting my eyes with hers, that before long I forgot all about being bashful.

We danced together some more and then she got took away from me to be partners with some other feller in a set. I stood by, watching them make up the squares, admiring how she looked and hating that feller that was with her. Then I seen Chino.

I realized I'd got so involved with talking to Annie I'd pure forgot about him. I hadn't noticed him in the dancing before, but there he was now, standing up next to Buell Stanhope's daughter.

He didn't look none too comfortable. He darted his eyes like a green horse in a strange place and shifted his weight from foot to foot. When the dancing started I could see he hadn't had much practice at it. He didn't seem to know most of the calls. But he was quick and light enough of foot to follow and he moved in the same easy way he did when he was working the horses, so he got along all right. By the time the set ended he'd got the hang of it and wasn't near so tense.

When the music stopped and the squares broke up, he had hold of Miss Stanhope's hand and he didn't let go of it. They walked off the floor together, both laughing like it wasn't at anything in particular but just for the fun they were having.

Annie Johnson left the feller she'd danced with and came back to me. And that was the last I thought about Chino for a while.

Annie and me went outside for some more punch. Seeing as how dancing got a person so warm and it was so hot up near to the barbecue pits, we decided we'd drift over and sit down on one of the wagon tongues. We sat there in the shadows, looking at how silver the snow on the slopes was in the moonlight and talking about all kinds of things. All the while it kept working in the back of my mind what I'd learned at the Arapahoe camp.

She gave a shiver and I asked was she cold. She said yes, so real polite I asked did she want to go back inside. But she said no to that. Before I knew it, I had an arm on her shoulder to keep the wind off her, though that wasn't the direction it was coming from.

My face was real close to hers and I was seeing just how full and soft her lips looked in the moonlight, and working real hard at getting up nerve to do something about it, when suddenly there come a shouting from the barn. It didn't sound like celebrating.

We both jumped and run to see what was happening.

The music had stopped. The people inside the barn were crowded back to the walls, leaving a clear space in the middle of the floor. There, in that clearing, I seen two men squared off to face each other. One of them was Chino. And both had knives in their hands.

I stopped dead, staring at them. Chino's face was dark and mean. His lips drawed back over his teeth like a wolf hungry for blood. He stood for an instant. Then he charged like a loco'd bronc.

The other man was a long, lean fence-rail of a feller who couldn't have weighed much more than Chino but he was easy half-a-head taller and he had the reach to go with it. From the way they moved even a green-horn could see neither one was a stranger to knife-fighting. And Chino was going for that feller like he meant to dig that blade into his gut and rip it right open.

He moved so furious that despite having the longer reach the other man wasn't able to do much but defend himself. More than once he just barely escaped getting Chino's knife in the soft part of his belly. He'd already caught it on his arm and there were drops of blood shaking off his sleeve when he jumped. He'd managed to put a few rips into Chino's shirt but I didn't see where he'd drawed any blood. He just wasn't fast enough.

The sheriff was at the edge of the clearing, hollering at the two of them. He'd been hurt a while back and was still lame, using a crutch to get around, so he couldn't do much more than holler. But a few of the cowboys set in to help him get it stopped. They circled the two fighters, looking for a way to break it up. Only whenever one would try to sneak up behind Chino, he'd wheel, slashing out with the knife so fast that they gave up that idea.

Nobody'd wore guns to the party but someone had run out to fetch one off his saddle. The sheriff took it from him and tried putting a couple of shots into the floor close to their feet. The skinny feller jumped and I could see he'd be willing enough to quit the fight if only he could. But Chino seemed bent on slicing him up and he just plain couldn't break away.

I couldn't believe what I was seeing. Chino was like a crazy man, the way he was going after that feller. He looked like he meant to kill.

From somewhere behind me, I heard somebody mutter ". . . devil when he's drunk." It reminded me of what Chino'd said to me on the ride over. I had the sudden horrible feeling all this was my fault for not watching out he didn't get to drinking. It was my fault and *I* had to stop it.

I took a step toward them, speaking out quiet but firm, the way I would to a randy horse. "Chino!"

He spun, swinging that blade at me, right

toward my bottom ribs. That instant his eyes met mine and I guess he seen it was me. His hand jerked, pulling back the knife as the point caught at my shirt. I felt it hook and tear, barely touching my skin.

Chino hesitated, looking startled. And suddenly two of them cowboys were on his back, grabbing at his arms. He slashed with the knife toward one. And the other slammed a big, knotted fist against the side of his head.

He went down, the knife sliding from his fingers, clattering on the floor. It sounded awful loud in the sudden silence.

I was shaking. I trembled like a bad-scared horse and felt like the bones inside me were crumbling away. The spot where that knife blade had touched my belly burned like fire, though it hadn't even broken the skin. And there was an awful hollow feeling in the pit of my stomach. I had a horrible notion I was gonna pass out like some fool girl. But then I felt a hand on my arm.

Swallowing hard, I stiffened my spine and turned to face the sheriff.

"You all right?" he asked me and I nodded.

I looked down at Chino. He was sprawled on his face, so limp and still that but for the stirring of his back as he breathed, I might have thought he was dead. One of the men knelt at his side and touched him.

"Out cold," he said, glancing up at the sheriff like he'd asked a question.

With a sigh, the sheriff leaned on his crutch and looked at Chino. "Take him back and lock him up. Lock them both up," he said wearily. Then he turned to me again. Like he already knew but wanted to hear it from me, he asked, "You're working for him now?"

I guess I nodded. My attention was on Chino. A couple of the men had hold of him and were starting to carry him off. I meant to follow after, but the sheriff's fingers closed tight on my arm, holding me back.

"You much help to him?" he asked me.

"I try to be," I mumbled, not understanding why he'd asked that and not much caring. My concern right then was Chino. "What are you gonna do to him?"

"Lock him up till he's sober. Tell him off good. Every time he comes to town he gets drunk. Damn near every time he ends up in a fight. Never before with a knife though." He shook his head sadly. "He's *gotta* learn better or he's gonna someday find himself with more trouble than he can handle. This could have been the time."

"Huh?" I grunted. The serious way he said that scared me.

"That damn knife. Judson pulled his first, but if Chino'd killed him, he'd have trouble on his hands anyway. Big trouble."

"Chino wouldn't kill anybody!" I hollered. But from the way he'd looked I wasn't as sure of it as I'd like to have been. It was like all the anger he'd held back when he worked the horses and all the meanness I'd ever seen, or thought I'd seen, in his face had all busted from inside him at once. It was like he wouldn't — *couldn't* — stop till he'd killed or was stopped hard, the way them cowboys had stopped him.

"Not sober, he wouldn't," the sheriff muttered. I knew then he'd seen it the same way I had. He still had hold of my arm, and he spoke to me quiet and serious. "Chino can't afford big trouble. And I don't want to see him get it. I got a good idea what kind of a job he's been doing up at the ranch. I know he's been on the square since he came to Colorado and I don't care what's happened before that. He works hard and he don't make trouble except when he's likkered up. But he come near to killing Judson and if he keeps up this way, maybe someday he will kill somebody. A thing like that happens, I ain't gonna be able to help him."

"It wasn't his fault," I said. "It was mine. He told me not to let him get started drinking."

"It was *his* doing. A man's got to be able to take care of himself. He can't look to somebody else to wet-nurse him."

I shook my head and repeated, "It was *my* fault. It's me you ought to lock up. Not Chino."

"That wouldn't do *him* no good," he said to me. "It's *him* has to learn. It's *him*'ll end up on the rope if he ain't careful."

I could see the sheriff had his mind made up. I asked, "Can I stay with him?"

He looked me square in the eyes. "You reckon that'd help? What about the ranch? Who's up there to look out for the stock? All them horses got graze? You got any idea how quick a horse'll gaunt without it eats?"

I thought of Banner waiting in the corral for us. The sheriff was right. My place was back to the ranch, tending the stock. As much as I didn't want to leave Chino alone in jail, I surely couldn't leave his horses without anybody to tend them. I nodded slowly. "I'd better get back."

X

The snow had begun again, but it was coming down softly and the moon gave a fair bit of light. I decided I'd ride Buck back instead of the sorrel. I was pretty sure I knew the way now, but I had a feeling old Buck would be wiser of the trail and of the night-traveling than me. Settling into Chino's saddle, I touched my spurs lightly to his flanks. He gave a snort and set out at an easy lope.

Miserable and worried as I was, I suddenly found I'd been asleep. I was lobbing over, halfway to falling out of the saddle. But Buck was ambling along, keeping a steady pace straight for the ranch. We were almost there and the eastern sky had begun to show signs that it would be sunup before long.

I wakened myself enough to turn him into the corral with Banner and fork them both some hay. Him and the colt greeted each other like it had been an awful long time since they met last. Then Banner come to me and looked all around, like he was worried for Chino.

After I'd got myself a couple of cups of strong hot coffee, I threw my saddle onto one of the using horses and rode out toward the *manada*. The sky was light by then and they were nosing around in the snow, digging out buried graze.

I rode around them awhile, trying to decide whether they were finding enough to eat or should be brought some hay. Chino'd be unhappy if I wasted it, feeding them when they could fare for themselves. But he'd be worse mad if I let them go hungry. It was hard to tell how they were holding their weight when they had so much shaggy winter hair on them and I didn't know enough to judge any other way. Finally I decided not to take any chances, so I went back and got the sled loaded.

Once I'd hayed them, I got to the rest of the chores, mine and Chino's both. It was my fault he wasn't there, and I meant to do all I could to keep things running right till he got back.

It was somewheres midafternoon when I heard a horse coming uptrail. It was Chino, I thought, my heart jumping inside me. But then I seen the red roan and recognized the man on its back as one of the sheriff's deputies.

"Where's Chino?" I hollered at him as he rode into the yard.

"In jail," he said. He drew rein and looked down at me curiously.

I felt the anger rising in me. Damn the law — they had no right to lock Chino up that way. I snapped at him, "What do you want here?"

"You getting on all right?" he drawled. His lazy way of speaking just made me madder.

"Yeah."

He just sat there and I wondered did he expect me to invite him down off his horse. Just let him try to set foot on Chino's land!

He asked, "You ain't need any help?"

"No!"

He lifted reins then and started to ride slowly across the yard, looking at the horses in the corral and then out at the *manada* where they were still working at the hay I'd given them. I chased after him, hollering, "You get off this ranch! We don't want you messing around here!"

He just kept riding, studying the place over.

"Git!" I shouted, madder than ever at the way he didn't seem to heed me.

He turned his horse then and faced me. Nodding to himself, he gigged the horse and started toward the ridge. Over his shoulder, he called to me, "Chino said there was

146

something in his saddlebag was for you. Said to tell you to help yourself to it."

I stood a minute, watching him ride off and burning inside. I was so tired and so mad I hardly noticed what he'd said. And it sure didn't occur to me I'd told him all the wrong things when he asked me could I handle the ranch alone.

It turned out the sheriff had been worried about holding Chino in jail any longer if it meant harm to the ranch, so he'd sent this deputy up to check on me and see just how bad I needed help there. When the deputy reported back what he'd seen of the place and how I'd answered him, the sheriff'd decided it wouldn't do any damage for Chino to stay locked up awhile longer.

Well, it had turned night and I was inside putting together supper of a sort for myself when I recalled what the deputy had said about something of mine in Chino's saddlebag. I went out and looked, but all I could find was that brown paper package he'd got in town. I took it back to the cabin and studied awhile before I decided to go ahead and open it.

It was a brand-new bone-handled sheath knife. When I seen it, I realized Chino'd meant it as a Christmas present for me.

I sat down on the edge of my bunk and

Banner came and put his head against my knee. For a long while I sat there, scratching his ears with one hand and holding the knife in the other.

I guess the little feller felt kind of lonesome. The cabin seemed awful empty without Chino. The lamp made a circle of light and the corners of the room were hollow and shadowy. Outside I could hear the wind coming down from the slopes and whistling around the corners. I could feel the chill of it through the chinks. Standing there with its bits of tin can and old rags for decoration, the Christmas tree looked awful strange. Not pretty or festive at all — just strange. It sure didn't feel like Christmas Eve.

After a while I got up and gave Banner some more milk. Then he climbed up onto Chino's bunk and curled up, tucking his nose under one foreleg. He'd slept inside plenty before, but always on the floor. Looking at him lying there, I thought he must miss Chino near as bad as I did.

I ate a couple of cold biscuits and some pemmican and then went back to work on my mecate. I had to get it finished before Chino come back. It sure wasn't much of a present, but it was the best I had. Only it was so smoky in that old cabin that my eyes blurred up and begun to water bad enough I could hardly see what I was doing.

Morning dawned cold and clear. I wakened lying across my bunk full-dressed, with the buffalo robe all twisted around me and no recollection of how or when I'd laid down.

I'd had dreams and they'd been mean ones. In them, Chino had come back all right but he'd found the stock all strayed and gaunted or else dead, and the whole place falling apart. Over and over again I'd dreamed he had turned on me and run me off the place on account of the way I'd failed him.

My head hurt and I felt stiff and weary but I dragged myself out and had some coffee. Then I went on with the chores, trying not to think how it was Christmas.

All through the day I kept looking up to the ridge, hoping I'd see Chino coming home. But night fell without a sign of him. The next day passed the same way and I kept feeling more and more miserable. I'd failed him and it was my fault he was in jail.

Another day come, chilly and gray. Along about noon the sun broke through the clouds but it didn't warm me any. Not deep inside where I was coldest. But then I heard the sound of a horse traveling fast, way off over the ridge.

It was Chino, I told myself. It had to be!

I swung onto Buck's bare back and kicked my heels into his sides, heading for the ridge at a gallop. I topped it just as Chino rounded the rocks. Spurring the sorrel hard he raced toward me.

"What's the matter?" he shouted.

I hollered out his name, so glad to see him again I could almost have cried like a girl.

He jerked the sorrel up by my side. "What's the matter?" he said again, hard-voiced, with his eyes narrow and mean.

I caught my breath and answered that nothing was wrong except he'd been away so long.

He didn't say anything to that, but just started the sorrel moving again.

Suddenly all my joy at seeing him back just crumbled away. What I felt was the pure misery of my guilt. Headhung, I reined Buck along at his flank. From the corner of my eye I took a look at him.

He seemed awful weary, with his shoulders slumped. His face was drawn and there were dark patches under his eyes and a thick stubble of whiskers on his jaw, like he'd come from long hard work without no rest.

Looking at him, I thought how a horse just in off the range will pace the fence rails when it's corralled. I had a notion Chino'd be like that in jail, fretting and pacing and worrying himself gaunt.

He didn't say anything more to me at all, but just rode on in, going around the corrals and then out to where the mares were working at the hay I'd given them. He sat watching them for a while. Then he headed back. In the yard, he stepped down and handed me the sorrel's reins. Still without speaking, he went into the cabin. I put up the horses and hurried after him.

He was sprawled on his bunk asleep, with Banner curled up on the floor beside the bed. The colt wasn't asleep but he looked like he thought he should be. When I walked in, he followed me with his eyes but didn't stir his head.

I went back out and messed around till suppertime. When I went in again, Chino was still asleep. I felt too low to bother with food, so I just bedded down. I slept restless and woke tired.

Usually Chino was up before me, but that morning I had coffee cooking before he stirred. He shaved before breakfast and he didn't look as weary as he had the day before, but he was still gaunt and silent. It seemed like we both avoided meeting each other's eyes.

I had got used to him having quiet spells when he wouldn't pay me much mind. But then he'd usually glance at me now and then and sometimes grin. This time it was different. I kept thinking to myself how I'd let him down. I was sure he was holding back from showing how mad he was at me, same as he held back when he got riled with the horses.

It wasn't till that night after we'd finished supper and I'd cleared up that I remembered about my mecate and how I'd meant to make him a present of it. I considered on it a long while, thinking how Christmas was past and how it was such a miserable little gift and everything, and I wasn't at all sure but what maybe I shouldn't forget the whole thing. I even thought maybe I ought to give him back the knife on account he'd bought it before I failed him. He might feel a lot different toward me now. But finally I got the coil of rope from where I'd hid it with a piece of that red rag tied in a bow on it.

Chino was sitting on his bunk with his shoulders against the wall, smoking and gazing off like his thoughts were a long ways somewhere else. I spoke his name but it come out so soft he must not have heard me.

Holding the rope in my hands behind my back, I shuffled over to him.

I held it out and mumbled, "Happy Christmas."

He took it from me, not saying anything at all. He didn't even look at me but just held the mecate in his hands, kind of staring at it. I felt myself flush all over at what a shabby present it was and how awful Christmas had turned out. I felt like shriveling up and blowing away. But I couldn't, so I turned around real quick. Grabbing my coat down off the peg, I hurried outside.

I walked over to the corral and leaned on the rail, looking at the mountains. With all that snow on the ground and a half-moon high up in the sky there was a lot of light. The air was clear as crystal and the whole world was silver and gray and black. The snow was so bright it seemed to be shining with a light of its own. And it was all cold and empty.

The sorrel geld nuzzled at my arm and looked at me curiously, catching pieces of the moon in his eyes. His breath on my hand was warm and moist.

Suddenly, without even thinking about it, I was throwing my saddle on him and mounting up. I set off at a lope, heading across the ridges where the wind cleared away the loose snow and the footing was good. I wasn't going anywhere in particular but just feeling the need of moving fast with a good horse under me.

It was like riding the wind. It seemed as if the geld felt the same as I did. I didn't have to tell him what I wanted from him. He flew along, skimming over the ground like his hoofs barely touched it. I let him have his head and just sat there, deep into the saddle the way Chino'd learned me.

The sorrel didn't slow till he was a mind to and then I didn't push him. I let him break stride and start to amble as he chose. That was when I discovered there was a horse following not far behind us.

I drew rein and turned in the saddle. There in the moonlight I seen it was Buck with Chino astride him bareback. He didn't have a hat or coat and I thought he must have jumped up and chased after me the minute he heard me ride out.

He reined down to a walk when I stopped and came up beside me slowly. I seen that there were pieces of the moon in his eyes too.

For a moment we sat silent, facing each other. Then, his voice real soft, he asked me, "You leaving for good?"

There wasn't any sort of accusation in the

way he said it, but I wondered if he thought I'd run off and steal the sorrel. Was that why he'd rode out after me that way? I swallowed hard and shook my head.

"If you want to go, you got the right," he said. "You ain't no way bound here."

Feeling low and miserable about how I'd let him down at the party, I thought that maybe this was his quiet, tightreined way of saying for me to leave. I didn't answer but just hung my head. The way the wind was stinging my eyes, they'd begun to water.

"I didn't do so good in town, did I?" he said.

It startled me — the way he said it. I suddenly realized he wasn't blaming me for failing him. He held himself to fault for what had happened — and he felt shamed by it.

I didn't know what to say. I shifted in the saddle and mumbled, "I ain't leaving. Not if you ain't sending me away."

"I'm glad of that," he said.

I raised my eyes up and looked him in the face.

He grinned kind of shy. "I've got used to having help on the place. You done real well by me while I was gone."

I grinned then myself. And we raced each other back to the ranch, whooping like a couple of wild Indians.

XI

After that night, Chino never mentioned the Christmas party or anything of what had happened and it wasn't till a long time later that I got up nerve enough to ask him what he'd been fighting about.

He looked at me kind of funny and answered that he didn't know. Then he owned as how after he'd sobered up he could never remember anything of what he'd done when he was drinking. He said he'd just waken in jail and know he'd got himself into trouble again and not even know how bad it was until the sheriff told him. Then he asked me if I'd seen whether or not Miss Stanhope seen the fight. I said as how it seemed like everybody was there, but I hadn't noticed her in particular.

He fell silent after that and I got to thinking on women and how much trouble they could cause. I didn't know whether Miss Stanhope had anything to do with Chino getting into that fight. But I felt real sure if I hadn't got all distracted by Annie Johnson I might have remembered my promise and might have stopped him before he got into trouble. I determined I wasn't having any more to do with women.

But a lot of times that winter, especially when I lay abed but wasn't asleep, I thought about Annie and about that Arapahoe girl and it would completely slip my mind how I'd swore off getting mixed up with women. I'd get to wondering when Chino meant to go back to the Indian camp and whether that girl would still like me as much as she had. I was real sure I'd still like her.

I asked him a couple of times about going back but he'd just put me off with some excuse or another. He didn't seem to favor the idea of going there again but he didn't say anything about it.

Winter got set in good and hard. Coming from the South like I did, I'd never seen such snow before. I'd never felt such cold either. It seemed to me this was a hard land, especially to be raising horses in. One evening after supper I asked Chino about it.

"Horses and men both — if the living gets too easy they get fat and lazy and not good for much," he answered.

"Is the living hard where you come from?"

"Well, the land's different. A lot flatter, except where it's cut into buttes and draws.

And the graze is a mite scanter," he said, keeping his face solemn. "The critters don't get enough meat on their bones to make it worth while for the buzzards to fly down at 'em when they die. What water we got is only what we squeeze out the rocks, and that don't work except in the wet season. Come summer the sun'll ketch fire to what wood it shines on and you got to mind your saddletree don't blaze up while you're riding. But in the winter there ain't no snow to worry over."

I could figure just about how much he was putting it on for me. Even so, it didn't sound very pleasant. I asked, "Is that why you left there?"

It was a minute or so before he spoke up, sort of thoughtful, "Yeah, I reckon so. It was just too damn hot for me."

When I asked him did he ever get a notion to go back he didn't answer at all. I'd got used to that by then though. If he didn't want to answer something, he just plain wouldn't. And he could change mood suddener than spring weather.

A lot of times during the winter he'd turn quiet that way. We didn't have much out-door work, what with all but the using horses turned out to range and the weather as hard as it was, so we spent a lot of long hours inside the cabin. Mostly Chino was real good company, learning me to make things out of leather or horsehair and telling me stories and such. But every once in a while he'd get to gazing off at nothing in particular and I'd know it was best I just left him be.

That ain't to say we loafed through the winter though. We had to keep mind of the herd and keep them hayed. And Chino had traplines set out that had to be tended. Sometimes he made the trip afoot on snowshoes. He brought in a fair few pelts and learned me to dress them. He even gave me some so I could make myself mittens.

When the weather was fit, he took me along to check the traps. He took me meat hunting, too, and I brought down my first buck.

More by luck than anything else, I hit it first shot. But I'd got so excited I pumped the Winchester empty. When I calmed down again I thought how much ammunition I'd wasted and how several times Chino'd said that cartridges didn't come cheap. I was pretty much ashamed. But when I tried to make an apology to him, he just laughed and told me the hide was mine and if I really wanted it all that full of holes he guessed we could stand the expense this once.

He made me do the gutting and skinning, though he did help me out and tell me how. Once I had the hide I asked him if maybe I could take it to the Arapahoe and get them to make me leggings like his from it. But he got quiet again and put me off from going back to the village. Instead he said he'd show me how to make them myself.

Well, what I had when I finished wasn't anywhere near as nice as his and didn't get any fancy beadwork on them. I hadn't been able to get big enough pieces that weren't perforated so I ended up with a couple of bulletholes in my leggings. But they worked and I wore them for years afterward before they begun to give out.

Everything went along right well, despite it being an uncommon bad winter. Spring got started eventually and the herd begun to move away from the cabin. Banner was growing into a rangy colt and turning the same color of blood bay as Flag. He ran off with the herd most of the time, playing and mock-fighting just as wild as any of the rest of the young colts, though they were mostly several months older than him. But every once in a while he'd cut loose from the *caballado* and come running back up to the ranch to hang around and watch the work and get in Chino's way. Sometimes he'd come at night, begging to be let into the cabin. He was getting pretty big for that but like as not Chino'd let him in anyway.

For a long while the trail had been snowed so deep it was impassable. But after the thaw started and the streams were running crazy with melted snow, a buckboard came rattling up to the place.

It was Stanhope and his daughter was with him. I could see from the mud on the buckboard it had been a hard trip. Stanhope didn't look very happy. He kept muttering about how his girl had carried on all winter with being anxious to see her horse and how she'd made life unbearable since the thaw began.

She just smiled though, looking funny at Chino. And he smiled back at her.

We'd brought the green horses in by then and the filly was with them. He'd been working her under saddle and she was going so nice in hand that he had me saddle up and ride her a bit.

Then I switched my kack for the sidesaddle they'd brought up in the buckboard and Chino made a step with his hands so the girl could mount up. She turned out to be able to ride well enough, though she sure wasn't any expert. Still, Chino suggested as how she might like to come take a few lessons.

Well Stanhope answered that before she could even get her mouth open. He said they'd take the filly back with them and that his daughter could learn her riding down to town. Plenty of fellers around there who could give her lessons, he told us.

I was glad of that. I figured we were gonna be busy enough without any woman coming out to get in our way. But Chino seemed disappointed. He switched his quirt against his leg but he didn't say anything. And when Stanhope drove off with the girl beside him, Chino and her exchanged glances like there were secrets between them.

Bedamned if she didn't show up at the ranch about a week later, riding the filly and all by her lonesome. Next thing I knew, Chino'd saddled up and they rode off together. I had a feeling her father wasn't gonna take too good to her doing that but maybe he never heard about it because she came back again the next week.

I didn't see her after that for a long while and I didn't pay any attention to how Chino'd ride off and be gone all day every once in a while. He did that a lot anyway. It wasn't till a time later I happened to be riding out one day myself and I come across tracks. Chino'd learned me a bit about tracking and I stopped to look at them just for practice. It was easy enough to read Buck's sign. He was never shod but Chino kept his hoofs trimmed and rasped.

I seen where Buck had met with a shod horse and had traveled alongside it. I followed a ways just practicing signreading and made out the shod horse had been light and carrying a light rider. Then I seen where both horses had stopped and there were footprints in the soft ground where both riders had stepped down. One set were Chino's moccasins. The others were the tiny-heeled sharp-toed prints of a lady's boots.

They went off into the grass toward an outcrop of rock that overlooked the valley and then they came back. Both Buck and the other horse had left enough sign to show they'd stood waiting a long while, maybe several hours. I didn't have any doubt that the other horse had been that sorrel filly.

I didn't ask and Chino never said anything. But I had a feeling that more than a few of the times he rode out he met with Stanhope's daughter. And I kept thinking how back East a feller and a girl weren't ever supposed to go off alone together without they were married to each other. I wondered if maybe that was one of the things that was different out here. Back East it meant sure trouble.

The snows melted away and the grass grew tall and green in our valley. The *manada* moved on down out of sight and the spring foals came, long-legged lumps of baby fuzz that frisked around the mares' legs. I don't think I could ever have got tired of riding out and sitting on a slope watching them.

Chino felt the same way about it. Spring was our busy time of year, but sometimes we'd take off and ride out together just to sit and look at the horses. He'd get to talking free then, about the *manada* and about other things. Mostly he'd talk about his plans for the ranch.

It was one day when we'd rode out and were sitting up in the rocks with the sun warm on our backs and our shadows stretched out over the slope. The sky was a bright blue and the smell of the fresh, sweet grass was strong in the air. Chino got to saying how he meant to build a proper house on the ranch before long.

"A big place," he told me, "with a real kitchen and a parlor and bedrooms and all that kind of thing."

"What do you need with a place like that?" I asked.

He grinned and bit into a grass stem.

Then he said, "Wimmen set a lot of store by a fancy house. And you need room in a house for kids."

"Kids?"

Still grinning, he looked at me. "Yeah. Hell. I ain't so young and wild no more as I used to be. I get me a notion sometimes I'd like to be raising more'n just horses."

I stared at him, trying to see him the way I pictured family men. It wasn't cowboys and *mesteñeros* who had houses full of wives and children. It was businessmen in suits with ties to their collars and paunches under their vests.

He cocked his head a bit at the way I was staring and the frown on my face. Swinging suddenly, he poked me in the ribs and laughed. "You think I can't do it?"

"Ain't that," I mumbled. The idea seemed so strange to me. "It's just . . . Chino, you're not . . ." I fished around for words and finally came out with, "Maybe you ain't so wild no more but you ain't a tame old harness hack neither."

"Don't intend to be," he answered me.

I still had the image of round-bellied businessmen in my head. I said, "It ain't natural."

"What ain't?" He seemed downright amused at my solemn tone. Pointing toward

Flag where he stood watching over his *manada,* he said, "See that studhorse yonder. He ain't broke to harness but he's got him one whopper of a family. I reckon there ain't a critter of any kind in the world that don't sometimes think maybe a youngun of his would be something special. He wants to raise up a kid and learn him all he knows and then watch him go on after that to be something better'n his pa was."

"Huh?" I grunted.

"Sure. Every critter wants to throw him a colt and see it grow and figure there's still gonna be a part of him alive after the buzzards have picked his bones." He stood up and added, "You'll likely find yourself getting the same idea one of these days."

I wasn't at all sure about that. I didn't argue him but I kept thinking on it as we rode back. It was a lot of idea for me to handle then.

I don't know what line his thoughts were following but he spoke up suddenly, startling me. "If I get myself killed while you're still around, you see I get buried Indian-style, in a tree, will you?"

"What?"

He laughed like he hadn't meant to get so serious. "I just don't like the notion of nobody throwing dirt in my face," he said.

Then he kicked his horse into a run and we raced back to the cabin.

Those spring days were full of work. But with Chino and me both going at it hard we had us some free time left in the evenings. It was then I got to thinking more and more about the Arapahoe camp and how much I wanted to go back there. When I finally brought it up again, Chino told me that they weren't there any more. They'd long since packed up and headed on to their summer range.

I felt disappointed and empty and cheated somehow, like he'd done me wrong by not taking me back there before they left. But he seemed to have reasons for not wanting to go back himself. Finally I added things up in my head and got to suspicioning his reasons had to do with Walk-Away's daughter and Louise Stanhope.

Once I knew the Arapahoe girl was gone and wouldn't be back till fall, my thoughts started drifting to Annie Johnson again. I got to wondering what my chance would be of running into her if I happened to ride into town. I was sure there must be dances and such down to Jubilee but I didn't have nerve enough to say anything to Chino about it — not after what had happened Christmas.

Eventually it occurred to me that if he didn't mind my taking the time off I could ride into town or go to a social by myself and not even bother him about it. I felt pretty silly not to have thought of that sooner and I asked him could I take off to go to town the next Saturday.

He looked at me like he was studying on it for a while before he answered. All he said was *sure* but I had a feeling he was thinking a lot more than just that.

I rode into Jubilee on the sorrel with my spurs polished and my hair slicked and my hat cocked down over my forehead the way the cowboys did. I jogged up and down the main street a while, looking at the people, and then I heard the whistle of the train on its way in so I rode over to the depot to watch it arrive.

The sorrel was well-broke by then but he'd never seen the likes of a locomotive before and he went a little crazy at the sight. After I'd showed the folks that got out of the coaches a little Western-style riding, I got him back in hand and drifted around some more. I hadn't caught sight of Annie Johnson and I didn't have any business in town or any money to spend or even buy dinner and after a while I begun to wonder if I'd just been foolish coming in this way.

Feeling kind of disappointed about my trip, I turned my horse and headed on back to the ranch. It was fair late when I got in and Chino was already asleep. I was tired when I crawled into my bunk. But I laid there a long while just feeling lonesome before I finally fell asleep.

I guess I was kind of quiet the next morning. And so was Chino. I noticed he kept looking at me like he had some thought worrying at his mind. Along about mid-day when I was working in the corral he walked over and leaned on the fence rails watching me.

I stepped over to him and, frowning a bit, he said, "Boy, I reckon I've done wrong by you. I didn't mean to but it slipped my mind."

"Huh?"

"It's way past the best hiring time on the beef ranches around here. If you mean to find yourself a paying job, you should have moved on a good while back."

I understood what he meant about it had slipped his mind because it had mine, too. I'd been working on the ranch and it had come to seem like the natural way of my life. When spring came and we got busy I hadn't had a thought about leaving but only about doing my part here.

Chino was saying, "Working for found's all right to get you through a bad winter. But come summer I reckon a feller wants some coin in his pocket when he rides into town."

Likely that was true. Maybe I'd have felt different about my trip into Jubilee if I'd had money to spend. But I didn't want to leave Chino's ranch. I felt like this was where I belonged. It was home to me, more than any other place had ever been.

Real thoughtful, almost as if he was talking to himself, Chino said, "Well, you learnt me one thing this winter, boy. You showed me just how damn much trouble it is breaking a hand in to my way of doing things and getting him to understand my way of working horses."

I swallowed hard, not sure just how he meant that. I knew I'd been a bother to him a lot of the time, but I figured I was help enough the rest of the time to make up for it.

He went on in that speculating way, "Year or two from now I'm gonna be hiring me a regular hand and I'm gonna have to go through all that same damn trouble again." Then he looked at me kind of sidewise. "You know, if you was to hire on cheap enough, it might be worth the cost of putting you on now just to save me going through all that again with some different feller."

I let out a sigh and I could feel my grin crawling toward my ears. But I didn't stand a chance of holding it back. I got my tongue straightened out enough to work and I answered him, "A dumb, green kid like me likely ain't worth no more than you'd pay."

He grinned then himself. Moving sudden, he swung his hand through the fence rails and poked me in the ribs so's I jumped like a spooked colt.

"Ten bucks a month and found. That's the best I can do," he said. "I spent half of last night figuring and it's the damn best I can afford right now."

"Ten bucks!" I echoed, thinking it was a fair good piece of money.

He forced a frown onto his face and looked at me hard and critical. "You reckon you're worth it?"

"Just the hide and tallow are worth ten bucks," I said, looking for a chance to poke him back. He could almost always jump faster than I could count a coup on him.

Grinning again, he snapped, "There don't nobody get no tallow on working for me. I'll see to that."

"Yes sir!"

"Well now, that's settled," he said, "what the hell you mean leaving off with them horses to waste all day jawing over a fence?"

"Yes sir!" I gave up my notion of poking him back and wheeled sharp to get on with cutting out a handy-looking bay geld that I had an idea might turn into a good working horse.

He stalked away then, like he was hurrying to tend to something important. But I noticed he stood awhile in the shadow of the cabin, watching me work with the bay, before he went on to his own chores.

XII

Chino didn't keep cash at the ranch. He didn't even keep a few cents in his poke. Stanhope handled all the ranch's money and paid up all the bills. In town, Chino's word was good enough for any place he did business, except maybe the saloon. But when Stanhope next came up with supplies, Chino told him as how I'd been hired on for a wage and he was to bring enough cash to pay me whenever he came up.

Well, Stanhope made some sort of comment about Chino always saying *he* didn't need any help and flipped a gold eagle at him as if he always carried a fistful of them to toss around. He took to acting that way every time he came, showing off how casual he could lay those eagles around.

I know how that rankled Chino. He'd spent a lot of his life peeling snuffy broncs for a couple of dollars a head. And he'd worked hard building up this ranch that Stanhope would be taking profit from for no better reason than he'd had the money to put up for expenses and brood mares in the beginning. But he never said anything about it. He only switched at his leg with the quirt in that way of his when Stanhope was around.

Afterward though he'd get to talking about Flag. Every time Stanhope would rile him with that show of money, he'd start talking about Flag a little later. It meant a lot to him that Flag was his, free and clear. Even the partnership on the ranch was set up so Stanhope didn't have any claim on the stud-horse. But talking about Flag would some-times lead him to thinking about Banner.

He had to allow that Stanhope had legal claim to half-interest in the colt. That both-ered him a lot. Several times he approached Stanhope with the idea of buying full title to the little feller. He was willing to mortgage Stanhope his share of the ranch to do it.

Stanhope would discuss it with him and then say he'd think about it. The first couple of times I believed him and maybe Chino did too. But after a while we both come to realize he hadn't any intention of letting Chino get full title to the colt.

Stanhope had a resentment toward Chino. Maybe it was because Chino was a kind of man that he couldn't ever have been, no matter how much money he might own. It seemed like he'd look apurpose for weakness in Chino and when he found a soft spot he'd poke at it, always in snide ways. He'd mention that Christmas party or show off his money or say something else he was sure would gall him. And I'd see how every once in a while he'd dart a glance at the quirt flicking against Chino's leg, like it measured his success.

When it came to Banner — well, Stanhope knew how much that colt meant to Chino and just because of that I think he wouldn't have let Chino have full title for all the gold in Colorado. And there wasn't a damn thing Chino could do about it.

Well anyway, Stanhope handed over a gold eagle and Chino paid me with it at the end of the month and suggested maybe I'd like to take a day off in town to spend it.

When I rode off Saturday, he told me not to worry myself about getting back till the next day, if I was to take a notion to stay overnight. I didn't figure I'd want to, but when I got into Jubilee I found out there was a social that very night. I broke my gold-piece to buy a new shirt and britches and then spent some more to get a proper hot bath at the barbershop before I changed into 'em. Got myself a store-bought haircut, too, with fancy-smelling slick'um on it. I had hopes of seeing Annie Johnson at the social and I figured all that fanciness would be worth the cost, if I did.

She showed up at the dance all right and we danced together and she was every bit as nice as I remembered her. But I danced with another girl there too. Her name was Beth Ann Tatum and she was as nice as Annie, though in a different way. She was small and gentle and she made me feel — well, strong and manly.

All next month back at the ranch I couldn't decide which one of them I wanted to think about most. I didn't realize it then but I got to running off at the mouth about them to Chino like there wasn't anything else in the world. I could start talking about anything else — like how the sick mare he'd brought in was getting along or how far I'd got with cutting shakes so we could put a real roof on the cabin before the fall rains started, or how the stove pipe was beginning to rust out at the wall — and every time without knowing how it had happened, I'd end up talking about one of those girls, or likely *both* of them.

He didn't have anything to say on the subject — not advice, encouragement or warning — but he'd grin at me like he understood exactly what I meant. I reckon he did, too, because he still kept riding off and disappearing all day, coming back at nightfall smiling kind of quiet to himself. But by then I was too much concerned with thinking about Annie and Beth Ann to pay it any heed.

I got to riding into town once or twice a month during that summer, going to dances and socials and running errands for Chino and sometimes just calling on one or the other of those girls. I even drove horses in, when we had to make a railroad delivery.

Chino never went along and I wasn't sure whether he really didn't want to or whether he was just worried about what kind of trouble he might get into if he did go. I didn't think much about it though. I was glad of any chance to get in myself. When the first snow came that fall, it got me right unhappy because it meant before long the trail would be snowed over and I wouldn't be able to go calling till spring.

Chino didn't take any pleasure in it either. And when the second snow fell, though it was just a light sprinkling, he got downright moody and sullen. He snapped at me a couple of times so sharp I felt like he'd whipped me. We didn't talk to each other at all during supper and afterward I got busy spinning yarn for a new mecate. He just sat at the table with his feet up on it and a coffee cup in his hand, gazing off into space. That was all right with me.

But suddenly he dropped his feet down to the floor and looked toward me with a frown. When I looked back though, it seemed like he wasn't seeing me at all.

"I'm gonna fetch her up here," he said.

"Huh?"

He focused on me then. "I'll have to move you out to the barn till we can get another room built onto the cabin. But it's the only way. I ain't holing up here all winter without her."

"I don't know what you're talking about," I mumbled.

"You ain't near as dumb and green as you were a year ago. You know damn well what I mean."

I had a notion I did. "Miss Stanhope?"

He nodded.

"You reckon Buell's gonna take to the idea?" I asked, hedging around what I was thinking. I was sure Stanhope wasn't gonna hear of his girl having to do with Chino — not if he found out about it.

"Buell ain't gonna have no say. If I marry her with a preacher and all that, it'll make her *mine*, not *his*, won't it?'

"I guess so," I answered. It sounded right but I didn't know much about such things.

"Will he let you marry her?"

"He ain't gonna have no say."

"Huh?"

He leaned toward me and said, "Look here. When a mustang stud wants him a ranch mare, he don't go asking the rancher, does he? He just helps himself."

That sure shook me. I swallowed hard and said, "That ain't right! Not for people."

"What the hell you know about it?" he snapped at me. Then he walked out of the cabin.

I sat there a couple of minutes, all confused by what he'd said. It sounded to me like he meant to steal her, the way Indians steal women. And I don't care how far from Eastern manners we were, I was sure white men weren't gonna abide that kind of thing.

I was still sitting there when suddenly the notion come on me that he might be saddling up to go after her that very minute. I ran to the door and stuck my head out, but I seen he was only leaning on the corral rails looking off at the mountains. I figured he wanted to do his thinking alone, so I went back to working the horsehair. I kept telling myself that he was thinking it out and he'd sure come to see that it would be wrong. But I wasn't very easy in my mind about it.

After a while he came back in and bedded

down. He didn't mention her again that night and the next day things went along about the same as usual. He was still moody and didn't talk any except about work. I realized he was still thinking on her. I wanted to try talking him out of it, but I'd come to know by then that once Chino got his mind set on a thing no amount of arguing was gonna change it for him.

Along about midafternoon, I seen him go into the cabin. When he come out he was shaved and the collar of his good shirt was showing at the neck of his jacket. I knew where he was going and I was afraid nothing I could do would stop him.

I dropped what I was doing and went to fling my saddle onto the bay geld I'd took to using for a riding horse since we sold the sorrel.

Chino'd saddled Buck. He stepped up and wheeled toward me as I was jerking up my cinchas.

"Where you think you're going?" he snapped at me.

"With you," I said, not looking up.

"Like hell. You think I want company?"

"I think you might need help," I answered as I swung onto the bay. If I couldn't stop him, I was sure gonna stand by him.

We looked at each other face to face and

he said, "I don't *need* help from nobody. 'Specially I don't need help for nothing like this." With that he flicked his quirt against Buck's flank and took off.

"Chino!" I hollered after him. I held back the bay, thinking if he wouldn't agree to me riding along, I'd follow at a distance.

Maybe he understood how determined I was, because he drew rein, wheeling Buck in a half-rear. I'd never seen him so heavy-handed with Buck before. "All right," he called, his voice sullen. "You can ride along, maybe keep watch. But you ain't gonna interfere."

I loped up to his side, but I didn't say anything. He didn't either and we rode on toward Stanhope's.

It was late and shadowy twilight when we got within sight of the house. I was feeling real uncomfortable and a mite scared by then. I had a notion Stanhope wouldn't hesitate to shoot either one of us if he found out what Chino was up to.

We turned off the road and went through the woods behind the house. We dismounted there and Chino walked off with me following. He didn't make a sound moving through the woods but I kept stepping on things that cracked under my feet. Each one sounded as loud as a gunshot to me. At the edge of Stanhope's yard, we hunkered down to wait.

It seemed like an awful long time we waited there. Then the back door opened, dropping a long square of lamplight in the yard and I saw the girl framed in it. She had a dishpan in her hands and was about to fling out the water when Chino gave a hoot like an owl.

I saw her hesitate, her shoulders stiffening like she'd been startled. She looked around, though I'm sure she couldn't see us in the shadows. Then she gave a little nod and went ahead with emptying the basin. She turned back into the kitchen, closing the door behind her, but Chino didn't seem bothered. He still didn't move.

We waited some more and then the door opened again. This time the girl stepped out and strolled into the yard. Chino rose up and took a step forward so she could see where he was. She ran to him and as they met he pulled her back into the darkness of the woods with him.

He whispered something and I heard her answer in a shocked voice, "No, Chino!"

He spoke louder this time and I could make out the words, "Why not?"

"My father . . ." she protested, but he cut her short.

"To hell with your father. You're mine and you're coming with me."

Then he was leading her through the woods back to where the horses were. He stepped up onto Buck and held a hand out to her. She didn't seem to understand what he meant by it, but he took hold of her hand and hauled her up behind him so that she was sitting astride the horse with her skirts up over her ankles.

When we reached the road we set into a gallop. I seen her gripping her arms around his waist then, but it looked to me like what she meant was to hold on and not anything else.

Chino was grim-faced and quiet and I think he knew as well as I did that what he was doing wasn't right. But he was determined. It was Louise Stanhope he wanted and he meant to have her, same as he'd meant to own Flag and to have the horse ranch. He knew he couldn't buy her or earn her with work so he was taking her the one way he knew how — right or wrong.

She looked pretty grim, too. She looked scared close to fainting and I wasn't sure whether it was her father she was so afraid of, or maybe Chino. I got to worrying over that. It seemed to me that if she felt about him the way a girl should about a feller

183

who's going to marry her, she should have looked happier than she did.

We went toward Jubilee and then cut off onto a side trail. It turned out to circle around the town so that we came down the back way, off the slopes and onto the outskirts. Chino headed for a little house set off a ways and separated from the nearest place by a fair stand of trees. As we got closer I recognized it was Preacher Dodd's house.

"All right," Chino said to me as he halted in the yard. "You make yourself useful. You wait here and if anybody's followed us, you give a good loud hoot. You hear?"

I nodded and took Buck's reins as he helped the girl down. I was still feeling miserable about it all and right spooky. The moon was bright so I moved the horses off to the edge of the woods to wait and keep watch from the shadows.

The preacher and his wife must have been bedded already. I didn't see any lights in the house and it took a long time from when Chino started knocking until a light showed in an upstairs window. It took another long while before a light showed downstairs and then the door finally opened. When Chino went in, leading the girl by the wrist, I backed the horses till I was even with a parlor window. The blind was up and I could see right in.

I got a glimpse of the preacher with a robe on over his nightshirt. And I seen Chino. There in the lamplight his eyes were narrowed and his face mean, the way I'd seen him that first night I'd gone to the ranch. I hadn't seen or at least hadn't noticed him look mean like that in a long while.

I begun to feel a sort of sympathy for the girl. It was no wonder she was scared. No matter how well she and him might have got to know each other riding out together, and no matter how much she might truly love him, she was Eastern-trained, like my sister, and it must have come as an awful shock to her, having him steal her away and look as mean as that at her.

I still didn't like none of what he was doing but I told myself that maybe it would work out all right. If she truly loved him and would stand by him, once they were married and he was her lawful husband, there wouldn't be anything Stanhope could do about it. Not any more than Chino could do about Stanhope owning half-interest in Banner.

It wouldn't be bad having her at the ranch either, I thought. She could do the woman-chores and leave me have more time to work the horses. I got to thinking on Annie and

Beth Ann and I smiled at the notion that maybe I'd be bringing a woman up to the ranch before long myself — once I made up my mind which one of 'em it should be. But I surely didn't intend to steal her in the night like Chino was doing.

I seen through the window that the preacher had gone off upstairs, likely to get some proper clothes on. I glimpsed a shadow cross between the upstairs lamp and the window blind a couple of times. Seemed to me like he was taking a long while getting dressed though.

All this waiting had begun to wear at Chino's nerves. I could see him pacing inside the parlor. From the twitch of his shoulder, I guessed he was slapping at his leg with the quirt. The girl just sat there on the sofa, her face stiff and her eyes following him.

Finally the preacher came down again. He looked pale, like that mean look of Chino's had bothered him too. He crossed out of my vision and I backed the horses a bit more so I could see him. He reached out toward the girl and in a minute I seen her and Chino standing beside each other. I moved the horses a bit further and I could see the preacher in front of them with a book open in his hands. It seemed to be trembling.

Maybe if I hadn't been paying so much attention to what was going on inside I would have heard the horses. But I wasn't aware of anything except the people in that room until suddenly a voice came from behind me, "Keep quiet, boy, and you won't get hurt."

Startled, I turned in the saddle as he brought his horse up beside me. Somebody else moved up on my other side. I didn't recognize his face, but I only seen it for a moment. My eyes went right down to the barrel of the big Colt revolver he was holding pointed at my chest.

I meant to hoot and warn Chino. I really did mean to — but I was scared bad by that gun. Before I could work my voice up the one who'd come behind me had my neckerchief and was stuffing it into my mouth. Then he got my hands and tied them behind my back.

"He ain't armed," the man with the revolver said in a hoarse whisper.

The man behind me answered, "You stay here and watch him anyway."

There were more than just the two of them. There were six altogether and one was Buell Stanhope. I sat there, tied and gagged and helpless, with the one holding my reins and keeping that revolver leveled at me while the others walked softly toward the house.

Some of them seemed familiar, like maybe I'd seen them around town, but I didn't know who they were. And I hadn't any idea how they'd got there. Maybe Stanhope had caught quick that something was wrong and had trailed us, stopping to gather a few of his friends for help. Or maybe it had happened some other way. I never did find out. But that wasn't what mattered.

The important thing was they'd caught us — they'd caught me off guard and now they were sneaking up on Chino. It was my fault and there wasn't anything I could do about it now but sit and watch it happen.

XIII

Though the window I could see the preacher still reading out of his book. He jumped at the sound of the door being forced open. Chino wheeled and charged.

I couldn't see what happened then. I glimpsed a man rushing past the window and I seen the preacher stand with the book in his shaking hands, just staring. Then he lowered the book.

A few minutes later the men came back out the door. They were carrying Chino, limp as a half-sack of grain, and they flung him over Buck's saddle. I had a thought that he was dead, but then I seen his back move as he breathed. There was blood on his head and I guess somebody must have buffalo'd him with a gun barrel. Likely they couldn't have stopped him any other way short of shooting him.

Stanhope had his arms around his daughter and she had her face pressed into his shoulder. She was holding onto him and crying hard and I could see that any thought she had was for herself. At that moment I hated her. This was *her* doing. She'd made up to Chino — she must have what with meeting him all through the summer and giving him the notion to marry with her. But now there she was hanging onto her father and crying and not paying any mind at all to Chino unconscious over his saddle with blood in his hair and God only knew what was gonna happen to him on account of he'd loved her.

Stanhope left her there with the preacher and mounted up. We rode off, one feller holding my reins and another leading Buck.

I couldn't do anything. With that gag in my mouth I couldn't even ask where we were going or what they meant to do to us. I just sat there, feeling the horse moving under me, and looking at Chino with his head hung down and the quirt that was still looped on his wrist dragging in the mud.

We went back uproad and I thought for a while they were taking us to the ranch. But then we turned off and went a good ways into the woods. When we finally stopped I knew we were a long distance from anywhere. There wasn't a house out this way for miles.

We'd come up in a little park among the trees and the moonlight come down bright on us. But Stanhope's face was shadowed as he told the men to dismount.

One of them gave me a hand off my horse while a couple of the others pulled Chino down from the saddle. He was still unconscious. They held him up between them for Stanhope to look at him.

Stanhope jerked the quirt off his wrist and slapped it against his own leg, the way Chino always did. From the way he winced, it must have stung him through his britches. He stood considering for a while and finally Chino moved his head.

His eyes opened and the moonlight caught on them, like sparks of light shining off obsidian. He seen Stanhope and he twisted against the grip of the men holding him. But I could see there wasn't any strength in the move. The blow on the head had done hard by him.

Stanhope slapped the quirt against his leg again, only easier this time. He smiled as he said, "Strip the shirt off him and tie him to one of these trees."

Chino tried to struggle against them but it was no use. They pulled off his coat and shirt and shoved him up against one of the pines with his face to it. It was a big old tree, thicker around than his arms could span. His hands didn't quite meet when they pulled them around it and lashed his wrists with rope. They pulled the rope so tight he couldn't move.

Even when Stanhope slashed the quirt across his back, leaving a stripe of blood that looked black under the moonlight, he couldn't move. His shoulder muscles bunched and his head jerked. But he couldn't move at all away from that knife-sharp whip.

They held me by the arms. I don't know what I'd have done if they hadn't, but I started to lunge before they caught hold of me. I guess if I could have, I'd have kicked Stanhope down and trampled him like an angry bronc. But they held me and all I could do was watch as he lashed at Chino's back with that whip that could cut through horsehide.

Chino never hollered, though Stanhope kept on until his whole back was black with blood and his legs had gone limp. Then his head lobbed down onto his shoulder and I knew he was unconscious. That was when Stanhope stopped — when he knew Chino couldn't feel it any more.

Throwing down the quirt, Stanhope turned toward me and said in a stone-hard voice, "You tell that damned half-breed woods colt if he ever so much as speaks a word to my daughter again I'll show him good. I won't stop next time till he's dead! You hear?"

If it hadn't been for the gag I'd have spit in his face. I wanted to do that almost as much as I wanted to tromp him underfoot. His no-good, miserable, she-bitch of a daughter wasn't fit to even make moccasins for Chino Valdez. I wished to hell I'd been free to tell him so.

They mounted up, leaving me stand. I tested the thong that held my wrists tight behind me and then tried to get my fingers over the handle of the sheath knife on my belt. I panicked as I realized I couldn't reach it.

But as the riders started up, one of them wheeled around back of me. He jerked the knife out of the sheath and stuck the handle into my hand.

I sawed at the thong as they rode off, cutting into my wrist at the same time but not caring. As they left I seen they were leading off our horses. The goddamn bastards were leaving us afoot.

It seemed an awful long time before the thong finally gave and my hands were free. I jerked the neckerchief out of my mouth as I ran over to Chino.

I seen his fingers move as I hacked at the rope holding his wrists. When it jerked apart they dug at the bark, scraping over it as if he were trying to hold himself up but couldn't. He sunk onto his knees as I stepped to his side. With his chest against the tree, he raised up his head enough to look at me.

Hunkering down, I asked, "Are you all right?"

I guess it was a silly thing to say. But he answered me, "Yeah."

Then he slid his arm from the tree onto my shoulder and over it. With almost no sound to his voice, he said, "Help me up."

I got to my feet slowly, holding onto his wrist, and he rose with me. He did it, though I could feel there wasn't enough strength in him for him to do it.

"I'll get the sheriff," I said. "I'll get you to town to a doctor."

"No!"

"Chino, you're hurt bad. I gotta get you help!"

"No!" he repeated. "Not town . . . not the sheriff . . ."

I tried to tell him. I knew a man could die from the kind of beating he'd taken. I had to make him understand. But he just kept saying it over and over and then I felt him go limp against me as he went unconscious again.

I stood there, holding the weight of him

braced against me, not knowing what to do. Stanhope and his men had left me so's I could get loose. But they'd taken the horses and this place they'd left us was a damn long way from anywhere. They hadn't meant to harm me, but they didn't give a damn whether Chino lived or died. And he would die if he didn't have help. I felt awful sure of that.

The closest place was our own ranch. I could get a horse there and ride on into town quicker than I could walk back to Jubilee.

I eased onto my knees and let him down to the ground where the pine needles were thick and soft. He moved his arm, trying to hold himself up but he hadn't the strength and he sunk down onto his face.

"Chino?" I said, not sure whether he was really conscious or not.

He tried to lift up his head.

"I'm going to the ranch for a horse," I said. "I'll ride for help. I'll be back quick."

"No!"

I could barely hear him. Bending close, I protested, "Chino, I've *got* to get help!"

"Not town," he whispered. "Not those damn *veho* . . ." And then he was unconscious again.

I remembered that word. He'd used it a

couple of times before. It was a Cheyenne name for white men. It meant spider.

As I looked at his back I felt myself getting sick. I stood up, fighting the feeling. His coat lay where Stanhope's man had thrown it down. I picked it up and laid it gently over him, hoping I wouldn't hurt him as I did it. Then I set off.

I headed for the ranch, running till I felt myself beginning to break down. Then I paced myself the way I would a horse, jogging awhile and running awhile.

I was close onto falling when I reached sight of the cabin. Somehow I kept on going. There in the yard I seen Buck and the bay, both still saddled, with the reins knotted up on their necks. They'd been turned loose and had gone home.

When he seen me Buck started toward me, giving a nicker to be unsaddled and fed. But I grabbed the horn and dragged myself onto his back. Slapping his flank with the reins, I slammed my heels into his sides and headed off at a wild run.

Buck was a long ways from being the fastest horse on the ranch but I don't think there was another horse we had broke to saddle — or maybe not another horse anywhere in the world — could have gone the way I drove Buck that night. I hadn't a thought in my head about sparing him or pacing him. Maybe if I'd felt him weaken under me or stumble or start to fail, I'd have eased up. But he never set a hoof bad or broke stride. He just stretched out his stubby mustang neck and grabbed the wind through his nostrils and ran.

We went downvalley, across the good level open park where the footing was easy and the ground soft, up onto the ridges where the rocks are rough and hard and twist under hoof, and down again onto slopes so steep he had to set back and slide them on his haunches. And at the bottom he was running again, every rawhide muscle in him driving those pounding legs.

His flinty hoofs rang on the rocks as if he'd been ironshod. They hammered down so fast one after another you couldn't have counted his strides. The sound of them rolled, like thunder.

I didn't pick a trail. I drove him in a straight line. He went through the cricks without a change of stride, hoofs throwing water up onto my legs. And he went through the woods with me hugging his neck, the saddle horn pressed into my belly, to keep the low limbs from lobbing my head off.

The moon swayed in the sky. The world spun past me like the wheels of a freight train. And Buck kept on, never breaking pace, never faltering.

It was still dark with just the first traces of dawn in the far sky, when I heard the dogs start yapping at the sound and smell of us. Moments later I was jerking rein within the circle of the Arapahoe camp. I set Buck back on his haunches with his forehoofs scratching at the air and long streamers of foam flagging from his mouth.

The dogs had said we were coming. Walks-Away was out of his tipi with his rifle under his arm, waiting. Others were up to meet us too. They bunched around us with guns in their hands. But Walks-Away held them back from me with a gesture. As he stepped to my side, I felt myself falling.

I slid out of the saddle, my knees bending under me. But his arm caught me. Then the Wrassler was there, putting a hand on my shoulder. I managed to keep to my feet. Leaning against him, I begun to explain. The words ran out of me like water over rocks, all jumbled and broken.

The few things in Arapahoe I'd learned from Chino were all useless talk about food and clothes and game. The only sign-talk I'd learned were greetings and things like that. And Walks-Away nor none of his people knew enough American to understand what

I was saying. But somehow — despite my confusion and being so tired I could hardly keep on my feet, despite my not having the words to tell him with — somehow Walks-Away understood I meant Chino needed his help.

He turned and said something to his people. There were murmured replies and they began to move. A woman come forward and held up a cup of water for me. I seen it was Walks-Away's daughter who wore Chino's buckle on a thong around her neck.

By the time I'd drunk of the water and caught my breath, the men had their horses. I grabbed for Buck's reins but Walks-Away stopped me. He'd seen what I hadn't — that I'd rode Buck down till he should have been on the ground with his sides heaving or maybe dead.

He gestured to show me he'd brought me a fresh horse. It had a saddle on it, and I grabbed the horn, pulling myself up. I glimpsed the woman leading Buck away as I jabbed my heels into the Indian pony's sides.

Walks-Away reined up on one side of me and the Wrassler on the other, with several more men trailing out behind us as we galloped off.

It was full daylight when we got to the

place where I'd left Chino. And he was gone when we got there.

I sat my horse, staring at the ground, not understanding. That was where I'd left him. Those dark stains on the pine needles were blood. That was where he'd been lying. There was the tree he'd been tied to and there was where Stanhope had tossed down the quirt.

But the whip was gone. And so was Chino.

Walks-Away dropped off his horse and hunkered down. He touched the ground, touched the bloodstains. Then he spoke to his son. As the Wrassler got down and knelt beside him, I swung off my mount. When I looked close I seen what they were talking about. There were marks, places where the pine needles had been disturbed.

We followed the sign with Walks-Away leading. We went downslope where there was underbrush among the trees. That was where we found him. He was lying on his face in a thicket. The coat was still over his shoulders. And the quirt was looped on his wrist. He'd got it back and then he'd crawled off. It was like he'd meant to hide himself the way a hurt animal will.

As we came up he tried to lift himself on his arms. He didn't have much strength for it. Getting his head up he glanced from one to the other of us. Then looking at me he said, "You done right."

The Indians didn't touch him but turned to hunt for straight saplings. He seen what they were doing and managed to say, "Don't need any damn travois . . . can sit a horse . . ."

Walks-Away seemed to understand it was him Chino had spoken to. He hunkered down and Chino said it again, this time in Arapahoe words. Walks-Away nodded.

Him and the Wrassler got Chino into the saddle on the pony I'd ridden. Once he was mounted it was like his strength begun to come back. When the Wrassler started to get up behind to hold him on, he stopped them of that too. I think he told them he could stay a horse himself. I didn't figure it was so, hurt and weak the way he was. Likely if it had been anybody but Chino he wouldn't have been able to do it. But once Chino got determined of a thing, it'd take hell to stop him.

Wrassler mounted his own pony and gave me a hand up behind him. We set off and by the time we got back to their camp, I found myself asleep with my head against his shoulder.

I wakened when we stopped but only

enough to remember what had happened and understand where we were. Everything I looked at blurred in front of me and I could hardly feel my legs when I stepped. But I wasn't worried about it. All I worried about was Chino.

We were at Walks-Away's lodge, though. He and his people would tend to Chino. And the Horse-Spirit would take care of him.

I let them lead me into the tipi and settle me into one of those little beds. They put a buffalo robe over me and next thing I knew I was sound asleep.

I reckon it was just a dream but the Horse-Spirit come to me there that night in the tipi. I seen him standing alone in the middle of a meadow that was red as blood. He was a man, dressed like the Arapahoe. I couldn't see his face but I could hear he was chanting some kind of a song. I knew without anybody told me that he was the Horse-Spirit and that it was a death song. The sound of it made me shudder like a cold wind.

Then there was a horse under him, sudden the way things happen in dreams. It was a big white mustang stallion and he wheeled it, riding across that horribly red meadow. The horse paced, both legs of a side moving together, but he skimmed over the ground faster than any ordinary horse could run.

Then suddenly it wasn't him any more, but Chino riding across the meadow on old Buck. He was sitting loose-legged with his feet out the stirrups, the way he did so often. I felt awfully glad to see him and I called out. But he didn't seem to hear me.

I began to run toward him, only I was afoot and I was stumbling. The red meadow seemed to grab at my ankles like thick mud. I kept hollering as Chino rode toward the ridge, but he never looked back. Then just as he topped it and was about to ride out of my sight he drew rein.

I called again, hoping he'd come back for me, but he only waved. And then he was gone.

XIV

I thought Chino was dead.

I wakened all covered with sweat but shivering just the same and I had a feeling my dream meant Chino had died. I lay there wrapped in the buffalo robe, staring at the bright blue sky beyond the smokehole of the tipi, but only seeing a recollection of that blood-red meadow.

Then I shook myself and sat up. It was like twilight inside the tipi. I glanced around, not seeing anybody. I felt godawful alone and afraid. Then I made out there was someone lying on one of the other beds.

It was Chino and I jumped up to run to his side. When I touched my hand to his arm, he stirred. I let out the breath I'd held caught up in me.

"Chino?" My voice broke as I said it.

He lay with his face resting on one arm, and he didn't move his head but only opened his eyes.

Hunkering down beside him, I asked, "How are you?"

"All right," he answered. "You hurt any?"

"No."

"The horses?"

I knew he meant the stock. The last cobwebs of the dream cleared out of my thoughts. "I'll go tend them," I told him, "But I'll come straight back."

"No. You stay to the ranch, look out for things," he mumbled. "I'll be there soon as I can." Then he closed his eyes again.

I went on outside the tipi. Not far away I spotted Buck tethered. He looked kind of shabby with his hipbones poking up under his skin like I'd run the tallow off him the night before. But when I walked over he lifted up his head and pointed his ears at me like he felt all right. I was about to pull the picket pin when I seen his hoofs. They were ragged and worn down and I realized that if I tried to ride him they were gonna pain him bad. I scratched his head and then left him to look for Walks-Away and try to explain I'd have to borrow a horse.

When I found him it didn't take but a little waving to make him understand. He called one of the horse boys and in a few minutes the kid was back with a good-looking speckled blue roan geld of the Palouse type. It didn't care much for Chino's saddle and hadn't never been broke to take a bit. But the Indians put a hackamore on it for me and after I'd said thanks and goodbye as best I could I set out for the ranch.

It was late night when I got there and I was plenty surprised to see lamplight inside the cabin. I dropped rein a ways off and pulled the Winchester out of the saddle boot. Holding it with my finger on the trigger, I walked up and pushed open the door.

There was a man inside — a lean, rangy cowboy-looking feller. He was sitting at the table eating a steak cut from off the venison Chino'd left hanging. He looked up, as surprised to see me as I was him.

"Who're you?" I snapped at him.

"I could ask you the same," he grunted, glancing at my gun.

"This here is Chino Valdez's cabin. Does he know you?"

"Buell Stanhope does," he answered. "He sent me up here to take care of this place."

"*I'll* take care of this place till Chino gets back," I told him.

He looked surprised again and mumbled, "Stanhope said Valdez wasn't coming back."

I kept my voice firm. "He said wrong then. And I don't need no help till he gets here."

He got to his feet and shrugged like he didn't give a damn either way. Glancing from my face to my rifle and then back again, he moved away from the table. He pulled his coat off a wall peg and slipped his arms into it. As he started through the door, I called after him, "You tell Stanhope if he tries sending anybody else up here to take Chino's place, I'll blast him before he can step down off his horse."

He looked me over again. "You're a tough kid, ain't you?" He sounded like he was trying to be flip, but like he might really believe it.

"Yeah," I answered. "I work for Chino Valdez."

He walked on out and I stood in the doorway watching as he mounted up and trotted off over the ridge. Then I poured myself some coffee and sat down with the Winchester across my knees. I wondered if Stanhope really did think he could take the place away from Chino. Well if he did, he was gonna do it over my dead body — and I'd go down shooting. I put the Winchester by the head of my bunk before I settled for the night.

I carried it the next day and kept it at hand while I worked around the place, in case anybody tried coming up. Nothing happened though, except it snowed a fair bit.

Day after that a rider came over the ridge. I recognized him as that deputy sheriff on the red roan. But I threw a warning shot at him anyway.

He started for his gun, but then he came on in with his hands high. I let him talk from the saddle, not trusting him out from under my sights. I guess I was still a bit mad at him for that business the year before, too.

He claimed he wasn't bringing trouble but only had come to see how things were getting on. He told me as how everybody in town knew what had happened except for what had become of Chino and me. When the sheriff heard he'd sent a search party to look for us, but by then we were gone and there'd been enough snow to cover our sign. Then that man of Stanhope's had got back into town saying I was at the ranch, so the deputy rode up to check.

He wanted to know where Chino was, but I wouldn't tell him. All I'd say was that he'd be back and till then I didn't need no help. I added that Stanhope had damn well better keep away from me if he didn't want a Winchester slug in his gizzard and that went for his hired men too.

He grinned like he wasn't too fond of Stanhope himself and said he'd be right pleased to deliver my message. Then he rode off.

After a couple of days more the snow had got deep and pretty soon the trail was drifted over enough I was sure there wasn't likely anybody else gonna push through till the thaw begun. I stopped lugging the gun with me every step I took then, but I kept it fairly close at hand.

Well, I was kept fair busy what with tending my own chores and Chino's. Graze got short early and I had to set in haying the herd. I loosed all but a couple of using horses and the Indian pony. The ones I picked to keep at the cabin were well broke to saddle but none of them was as wise and experienced as old Buck and I surely missed him.

Then one day the Wrassler showed up. He had Buck on a lead and a quarter of venison hung over his back. I was grateful for the meat. I'd managed to get the traps out and figured I'd be eating what I skinned, for I didn't have time to go after deer. And I was really happy to see that old pony again.

I tried to give the Wrassler back the blue roan they'd lent me. But finally he made me to understand it had been a present. Chino'd told me the Indians went strong for present-giving so I loaded him up with as much of our canned goods as I figured I could spare. I wrote a note for him to give Chino, too, saying as how he shouldn't worry 'cause everything was going along fine.

Myself, I didn't have time to worry. Nor to think much about Annie and Beth Ann either. I had my hands full. If there was a Christmas that year, I sure didn't know about it. I couldn't be bothered keeping track of the days and all I noticed was when the daylight started getting longer instead of shorter.

The weather was bad for a while and then broke good again. The ridges got clear enough that I could ride out most of the way. I was coming back after dark with a couple of pretty good pelts and I think I must have been dozing in the saddle because I was into the yard before I seen there was light in the cabin.

I reached for the Winchester, thinking Stanhope had moved in on me again. Then I seen one of the yearlings was up hanging around the cabin. Just as I recognized it as Banner, the door opened and I seen Chino silhouetted much the same as I'd seen him the first time I come there.

Grinning so wide my ears near cracked, I drew rein and called out, "Mister, you need any help on this here place?"

He cocked his head a bit and answered me, "From what I've seen, it don't look like *you* need no help on this place."

I swung down off Buck, feeling my legs like a couple of stumps under me. "I sure *feel* the need of help."

"Come on inside," he said. "I got coffee cooking."

I went straight to the stove and took a deep whiff of it. The cabin was all warm and cozy inside and that coffee sure smelled good.

Chino came over to the table, walking wearily and limping a little, like maybe he was still pretty sick. He swung out a chair and sat down astride it, putting his arm up on the back and resting his chin on his hand.

I poured coffee for both of us and then sat down across from him. His face was drawn and tired-looking, with the bone showing sharp under his skin. There were dark hollows under his eyes. He looked straight at me and I could see the reflection of the lamp in his eyes like there were little fires burning deep in them.

"How are you feeling?" I asked him.

"All right," he muttered. He sounded like he didn't much care.

After we'd both drunk of the coffee he

started in to asking me questions about the place and the horses and how things were going. As I answered him he seemed to start coming alive again. We got to talking on about plans for the spring work and about the colts and which looked to shape up into the best horses — which should be sold green and which held for training, and things like that.

By the time I bedded, I was feeling real fine. Chino was back and even if he was still sick from that beating he'd have his strength again soon. By spring everything would be back the way it belonged.

He was up before me the next morning and had the coffee started by the time I got my eyes open. He grinned and kidded me about hibernating and we both ate a good big breakfast. Then he took his coat down off the wall peg. There under it was the quirt. He took it off the peg and slipped the thong around his wrist. I seen the dark stains of his blood were still on it.

He glanced at me and saw how I was staring at that whip. For an instant his face was hard and mean and it seemed like there was fire burning in his eyes again. He started like he was about to say something to me, but instead he just flicked the whip against his leg and turned to walk out.

I told myself it was only natural he'd be carrying the quirt again. It was a tool he used in his work. But I had a feeling it was more than just that. It was like — well, maybe it was that Stanhope had whipped him like an animal with that quirt but hadn't busted him. Chino wasn't gonna cower and tremble like a scared horse at the sight of the whip.

Did he still mean to have Stanhope's daughter, I wondered.

I got busy enough that I didn't have much time for thinking about Stanhope and his daughter after that. For one thing, I got busy worrying about Chino. I tried to hold him back from working too hard but I might as well have argued with a fence rail. I knew he was still sick from that beating and I could see how he'd run short of strength. But still he'd keep going. The only way I could slow him down was by having chores done before he could get to them, and I drove myself to it.

In time though he begun to put on a little of the flesh he'd lost and to get back the strength he'd had. Things come to be so much like they had been, with him kidding me and learning me stuff and telling me about things he'd done and places he'd been, that the worries went out of my mind.

It got to where I even stopped noticing how he'd fallen into the habit of sitting astride a chair instead of leaning back with his feet on the table the way he used to.

Finally the worst of the winter passed. The horses begun to shed their long shag and started moving down valley toward the foaling place. They'd wintered good and from the look of the mares we were gonna have a real fine crop of colts this year.

There was a lot of mud and the trail up to the cabin wasn't yet passable to a wagon, but the spring sun was blazing bright and warm trying to dry it up, when I first spotted riders coming. I was up on the roof taking advantage of the sunshine to replace a few of the shakes the winter had tore loose when I seen them. There were three of 'em and I couldn't tell who they might be.

I stood up watching as they topped a distant ridge and then disappeared behind a closer one. Then I swung down off the roof to meet them when they rode up. Sight of them had reminded me that the spring might be bringing us trouble.

They paused on top of the ridge and I seen the one in the middle was Buell Stanhope. It didn't take but a glance to see he wasn't used to riding a saddle and didn't take too good to the idea. It was a slack-lipped livery hack he was astride and he looked like he'd had a hard trip up. The two men with him were riders though, and I couldn't help but admire the round-rumped gray one sat.

Stanhope sure must have wanted awful bad to get to the ranch to have traveled that way. I took a step forward, torn between wishing Chino was there and worrying that I wouldn't be able to get rid of Stanhope before he got back. But just then he come galloping into the yard like he must have spotted them riding up.

Stanhope hesitated at the sight of him but then he kicked at the hack's sides and came on in, leaving those two riders waiting up on the ridge. He rode in slow and by the time he reached the cabin, Chino had dismounted and was standing watching him.

I moved over to Chino's side as Stanhope drew rein. Whatever happened, I meant to stand by him. He didn't say anything, but just switched the quirt against his leg. And when Stanhope seen that a look came over his face dike he was about to dig heels into the hack's flanks and bolt away.

But he didn't. He sat there and drew a deep breath. Then, in a pleasant, drummer's voice, he said, "I come to talk to you, Valdez."

Chino looked at him without much expression in his face. There wasn't much in his voice either as he said, "Then step down and come on inside."

Stanhope glanced back at his men, as he heaved himself out of the saddle, but he didn't make any sign to them. Brushing at his wrinkled coat front, he followed Chino into the cabin and I tagged after them.

"What's your business?" Chino asked, his voice very soft and mild.

The sound of it seemed to ease Stanhope's concern. He puffed up a bit as he reached inside his coat and pulled out a poke. When he tossed it onto the table it clinked like coin. "Gold," he said. "The price of your share of the ranch."

Chino just stood looking at him.

"I'm buying you out," he explained. "That's a fair price — a damned fair price — and it's hard money. Should stake you to a good start wherever you want to go."

Still in that soft, mild way, Chino answered him, "I ain't going nowhere."

Stanhope looked bewildered. "But after what's happened . . ."

"Ain't nothing happened that had to do with this here ranch or the horses, has it? We got a *business* agreement, ain't we?"

"But . . ." Stanhope looked stymied. He

glanced around like he was trying to find something to fight Chino with. Then he sucked in his breath and let it out with a sigh. "Valdez, my daughter's gone back East."

Chino's eyes narrowed down, looking black and mean. "You sent her away?"

"She *wanted* to go." Stanhope sounded oddly like it hurt him to say that. "You scared her away. You . . . you . . ." He sputtered into silence.

For a moment Chino didn't move. Then, flicking the whip at his, leg, he said, "I got work."

He wheeled and walked out. Stanhope called after him but he just swung onto Buck and set off at a gallop. Stanhope stood in the doorway, watching as he rode off, and I seen his shoulders slump down and his face sag.

I asked, "Is that true? Did she really run away from Chino?"

He nodded. Then he gathered himself up, stiffening his shoulders and pulling his face back together. His voice firm, he said, "You tell him how it is. Tell him she don't want anything to do with him. She's scared to come back while he's still here. Tell him I mean to have her home again if I have to kill him to get rid of him."

I swallowed hard and asked, "Why'd she

do it then? Why'd she lead him on if she didn't care about him?"

He snapped it at me. "She was curious! She was amused by him. He was *different*. Different! Damn him, he'll be *dead* if he don't get!"

With that he stalked out of the cabin and mounted up. He rode off, flanked by those two hard-looking men.

Chino didn't come back that night. I lay awake through most of the night listening for the sound of Buck's hoofs. But dawn came without a sign of him. I went about my chores, telling myself it wasn't anything unusual for him to be gone overnight. Midday I rode out looking for his sign, but the mud was so sloppy I couldn't find anything to follow.

He was still gone the next night. Come daylight I fed the corralled stock and then saddled up my roan and headed for town. I didn't know what else to do. I meant to see the sheriff and tell him everything that had happened.

I met Chino on the trail up, and from the look of him things had gone hard with him while he was away. He barely glanced at me as I drew up by his side and asked, "Where you been?"

"Town."

"You been in jail?' I asked.

He nodded.

"Fighting?"

He nodded again.

"Chino . . ." I started.

"Leave me be, will you?' he snapped at me.

We rode quiet on back to the cabin. Inside, I built a fire in the stove and got coffee started as he sprawled out on his bunk. But this time he didn't fall asleep. He just lay there, looking at nothing.

When the coffee was ready I asked him did he want some.

"No," he said. But then he got up and come on over to the table. Settling himself astride a chair, he picked up the cup I poured for him and drank from it. Then he told me, "It was true what he said about Louise. I went to town to find out and it was true."

I nodded.

"I didn't mean to take her against her will," he said, sounding vague and puzzled. "She didn't understand that! She didn't understand anything!"

He shook his head slowly. "Why the hell didn't she say it? What's she scared of me for?"

"Because she's a goddamn feather-headed

fool!" The words come spilling out of me without I could stop them. But maybe I didn't try very hard. "You shouldn't have bothered with her. She ain't nothing. Just a dumb-headed, stallbred nothing!"

"Don't talk against her," he said quietly. "It's all done."

"No, it ain't! Now Stanhope means to run us out." I told him what Stanhope had said. I ended up, "Chino, there ain't any way this partnership between you and him can work now. Why don't you sell? Take the money and Flag and start up somewheres else."

"Let *him* have my horses? Let *him* have Banner?"

"He'll run you out . . ."

"I've been run by better men than him. I've been run by the Army, the Rangers, Indians . . . I've been run out of Texas and New Mex. You reckon a fat-faced bastard like Stanhope can run me? What's he gonna do? Whip me again? You reckon he can run me that way?"

"He'll *kill* you!"

The corner of his mouth twisted up a bit. His face looked mean and hard. "He ain't got the gut to kill a man."

"Chino . . ." I said. But I could see there wasn't any use in arguing him.

He got to his feet, standing straight and

looking tall. "I got horses to tend," he said. He started out the door. Then he looked back at me over his shoulder and kind of grinned. "Next time I get mixed up with a woman, it ain't gonna be one that won't admit she's got legs."

I grinned back at him, thinking there wasn't anybody or anything that could beat down Chino or turn him once he got determined of a thing. If Stanhope meant to have himself a war, he was gonna get it.

And he was gonna lose it.

XV

I guess I wasn't sleeping very deep. I came wide awake at the touch of Chino's hand on my shoulder. The shutters were open and from the moonlight I could tell it wasn't anywhere near dawn yet.

"What's the matter?" I muttered.

"Dunno," he answered hurriedly, "but something's wrong."

I'd taken to keeping the Winchester near the head of my bunk. As I grabbed for it I heard a galloping horse. From the sound, it was coming into the yard. I jumped, throwing open the door. I was just in time to see the shadowed form of a rider heading up the trail over the ridge. From what I seen, the horse looked like that round-rumped gray Stanhope's man had been riding. I started to run out, meaning to snap off a shot at him. But I stumbled and then he was gone from sight.

Catching at the doorframe, I looked to see what I'd tripped on. Chino lit the lamp and was carrying it as he came up beside me. The light spilled down on the head of a horse, lying on the ground. It was Banner.

I hunkered down, staring at the cold blank eye under the long lashes and at the hemp rope choked tight around the slender neck. There was no grace in the neck now and no spirit in the eye.

It wasn't the rope that had drawn the life out of the colt though. I seen the dark stain of blood on his neck up near the shoulder. And the small bullet hole that had spilled it out. Then I seen what had been done to him.

He had been butchered — cut apart through the barrel. What had been dragged up and left at our door was just his forequarters.

Chino knelt and held out the lamp. He reached out his hand and ran his fingers over the colt's face like he was feeling for some trace of life — like he couldn't believe what he was seeing. He scratched at the head up close to the ears. Then he ran his hand along the neck. By the lamplight, he looked at the still-damp blood that smeared over his palm. Deep in his throat, he said, "The half that's mine."

He stood up then and walked back into the cabin.

I felt sick — too sick to hold back. I went off a ways. When I got back, Chino was sitting on his bunk, leaning his shoulders against the wall. He had one knee up and his arm resting on it. He was gazing at his blood-smeared hand.

I spoke his name but he didn't answer.

At first I tried to ask him about what had been done and what we would do. But then I just tried to get him to answer me. Or look at me. Or show some sign he heard me.

Maybe he didn't hear.

Finally I sat down on my own bunk, sinking my head into my hands.

The sun come up. It rose over the ridges and the horses in the corrals begun to get restless and to nicker. Eventually I got up and went out to tend them. But Chino never moved.

I stepped over Banner's head. I couldn't look but yet I couldn't help looking and it was a lot worse by daylight. Flies had come too, and they swarmed over what was left of the colt. I couldn't stand that.

I waved my hands at them, shouting like crazy. Then I fetched out my buffalo robe and covered it to keep them off.

I didn't know what else to do. I went on and tended the stock. Then I went back to Chino. He still wouldn't answer me or look at me or show any sign.

I was sick about Banner. And I was

worrying-sick over Chino. But all I could do was wait for him. That was best done by working, so I set myself to the ranch chores.

It was along about midday and I was in the corral when suddenly I realized he'd come out of the cabin. I turned and seen him hunkered down, one hand holding the robe up off the colt's head while he studied it.

I went over to him but he didn't pay me no mind. After a couple of minutes he dropped the robe down again. Then he walked off. I followed along but I understood by then it wouldn't do no good to try talking to him.

First he saddled Buck. Then he cut poles and rigged a travois. He led Buck over and the old horse nuzzled at the buffalo robe, scenting the colt and the blood under it. But he didn't spook. He stood steady while Chino started trying to haul what was left of the colt onto the travois.

Banner had been close onto two years old then and fair good sized. When I seen what Chino was trying to do, I gave a hand. He didn't try to stop me helping. He didn't even seem to notice I was there.

We got the bundle onto the poles and lashed. Then he took hold of the bridle and led Buck off. Keeping silent, I followed along.

It was a good ways, especially afoot, but Chino never stopped or even broke pace. Not till he'd got back to that little park by the creek where Banner'd been foaled.

The sun was low down over the ridges by then. The light of it was a kind of orange. It made the woods and valley and mountains all look strange, like something from a dream. The mare's bones were still there in the clearing, with the spring grass poking up through them. In that light they looked like gold.

Chino stood studying for a moment. Then he led Buck off to the trunk of a big old pine. It had been hit by lightning once and split open about head-high off the ground. Part of it had broke and fell away at the split, but the rest still stood. There was a new shoot sprouting out of it.

Chino unlashed the bundle from the travois and it took me awhile to catch onto what he was trying to do then. But when I did, I set to helping. Using ropes and Buck to haul, we managed to get the bundle off the ground and up into the cleft of the tree trunk. Chino lashed it firm there. Then he dropped back to the ground.

He still didn't speak to me. But when he settled in the saddle, he held out a hand. I swung up behind him and we started back.

As we rode out of the woods onto the edge of the meadow, I seen how the sun was halfway down behind the far ridges and was as red as blood. The light it spilled into the valley gave the tips of the meadow grass a reddish color. I shivered, remembering the dream I'd had at the Arapahoe camp.

That night I bedded down but I didn't sleep very good. I kept wakening and when I did, I'd look at Chino. He was a shadow in the moonlight, sitting on his bunk the same way he'd done all morning.

Come dawn he stirred himself. He got coffee started and I got up and made breakfast, same as I did every morning. I tried saying something about the work we had, but he didn't answer me. I asked him what he was gonna do and he didn't answer that either. He ate with me, though, and then we both went outside.

He stood awhile looking at the horses in the corral. Then he asked me, "You want a Valdez horse?"

"Huh?" I didn't understand that at all.

"You've earned a damnsite more'n you've been paid," he said. "If you want a horse, pick the one you want. Any cayuse on the place except Buck or Flag."

There wasn't much I wanted more than a Valdez horse. My first thought was of a flash black three-year-old geld I'd been working with. But then something else come to me and I asked, "You're paying me off?"

He nodded.

"I ain't afraid of Stanhope! I don't want to leave. I want to stay here with you."

"I ain't gonna be here. If you want a horse, pick him now." His voice was quiet and strange, like something in a dream.

"Chino, if you're leaving, I want to go with you," I said.

Shaking his head, he answered me, "No. We ain't going the same way from here. Maybe we'll cross trails again someday. But right now we're splitting up."

From the way he said it, I knew there was no good arguing him.

I looked at that black geld in the corral but I thought to myself if I was leaving I wanted a mare — one with Flag's blood — that I could breed. That way I could always have me a horse that was at least part a Valdez horse. I muttered something about a good-sized white-face bay mare that was in the *manada*. She wasn't saddle-broke but she was fair tame, having been one of the first colts foaled on the ranch.

"She's a good choice," Chino said. "She's got a foal in her belly."

My heart jumped at the idea she'd drop a

colt sired by Flag for me. But then I said something about not wanting to cheat him by taking two horses for one. He answered, "You take her. You've earned more."

We saddled up, not talking, and we rode out, him on Buck and me on the roan the Arapahoe had given me. First we roped the white-face mare and then the old mare I'd rode in on when I first came to the ranch. She'd been running to pasture the whole time I'd been there and she'd filled out and perked up, showing there were a few more good years in her. I neck-roped the two of them together. Then Chino caught and haltered Flag. I asked him why but he wouldn't answer me.

We rode back to the ranch and he put Flag in the small corral, tying him by the lead rope. Then we went into the cabin. Chino sat drinking coffee while I made my bedroll, packing in the things I'd got since I come to the ranch. There wasn't much.

I went out alone and tied my bundle to my saddle. I didn't mount up though. I wiped at my eyes and stood there till Chino come out and said to me, real soft-voiced, "Jamie, you'd better get now. You ride off and don't come back, will you?"

I nodded and stepped up onto my horse. It was the first time since I'd been there that

he ever called me by name. Always he'd
called me *kid* or *boy*. I'd never minded because I figured measured to him that's all I
was. But now he'd called me by name like
he'd decided *boy* didn't fit me no more.

Feeling ashamed of how damp my eyes
were, I raised up my head and lifted reins. I
rode off, not wanting to, but it was what
Chino wanted and I didn't mean to go
against him.

I'd got a good ways along the trail before I
stopped. I couldn't go on. I couldn't leave
him like that. Only he had said for me not to
come back.

I circled through the woods and off up to
a ridge where I could look out and see the
cabin. I thought maybe I could follow him.
Maybe after a while he wouldn't mind my
joining him.

I seen Buck standing saddled near the
door. Then Chino come out. He had his
own bedroll and warbag and lashed them on
the saddle. He didn't have much gear either.

He turned loose all the horses we'd corralled. All except Flag. Then he mounted
up, herding them ahead of him. I rode along
in the edge of the woods, trying to stay hid
but still to keep him in sight as he worked
the horses down toward the *manada*. When
he had them all together, he made a wide

circle around, herding them in close. He had every horse on the place bunched there. Then he begun to move them up toward a box canyon we'd used for a corral when we were cutting and branding the colts.

I couldn't figure why he'd do that, or why he'd left Flag back at the cabin. I couldn't make sense of it at all when he drove the herd into that canyon and then rode away.

But he turned at the mouth of the canyon and rode upslope until he was on the edge of the ridge overlooking it. He dismounted there and pulled the Winchester out of the boot. Setting himself down, he braced the rifle, like for careful precise shooting, and aimed it into the herd. Then he fired.

I saw a long-legged young mare throw up her head and then fall.

He kept firing, fast as he could lever shells and take aim. The horses went down, one by one. Some just crumpled up and fell limp. But some screamed and I never in my life heard anything more terrible than that screaming. Even now there are times I hear those screams in my sleep. And I've never heard a horse scream since then but what I didn't remember that day and shiver at the memory.

The screaming and shooting and smell of death panicked the herd. They begun to rear and kick and mill, going crazy with their fear.

But Chino just kept firing. When a spooked horse would try to bolt out of the ravine, he'd aim for it. A few got through though, without him shooting at them. It took me a minute to realize he was letting them escape.

My horses had got frightened too and had begun to fuss. I guess my hands moved from habit, calming and holding them, for I didn't pay them any heed. I just sat there staring at what was happening.

Chino'd brought cartridges in his pocket and when the rifle was empty he reloaded quick and went on with his firing. He dropped three horses and then let two in a row escape.

I begun to see the pattern of it then. He was slaughtering the ranch-born horses and letting the old brood mares run free. The old mares were the ones he'd first stocked the ranch with — on Stanhope's money. The ones he was killing were Flag's colts, with the stud's blood in them. And Flag was his — all his.

He was killing the part of the herd that belonged to him.

When it was done — when the mustang mares had fled and the Valdez horses all lay twisted and limp with their blood staining the new grass — he got slowly to his feet. He walked back to Buck, moving wearily, limping a little. He shoved the Winchester into the boot and mounted up, turning toward the ranch.

I started to follow but my horses were skitterish and gave me some trouble. By the time I got them settled he was out of my sight. I struck for the ranch and when I topped the ridge, I seen him riding away leading Flag. Behind of him, I could see thin twists of smoke curling out the windows of the cabin and the doors of the outbuildings.

Chino was going. But he was leaving nothing of his — nothing of the work he'd done or the things he'd built — for Stanhope.

He rode onto the trail toward the main road and then he was out of my sight behind the ridge.

Until that moment it had been like some kind of a dream — like a nightmare — but right then I realized that it was real. Everything was over, my home on the ranch was gone. And Chino was gone.

I slapped my reins on the roan's flanks, hauling at the lead-rope I had the mares on. He'd disappeared over the ridge but he hadn't been traveling very fast. I was sure I could catch up to him.

I galloped hard but I didn't get a glimpse of him again. When I got to the main road I dismounted to look for his tracks and see which way he'd turned. But I couldn't find any sign of them. I rode back along the trail then, watching the ground for some mark of Buck turning off into the woods. I couldn't find that either.

It was like he'd never been there. But it wasn't a dream. Off in the distance I could see the smoke from the burning ranch buildings.

I searched for sign until there was no light left. Then I gave up and headed back for the main road. I understood Chino had hid his trail apurpose. I had a feeling he'd known about me when I was there in the woods watching him kill the horses. He'd let me follow him then. But he wouldn't let me trail him any farther.

Head-hung, I turned my horses back to the main road. I thought of going to Jubilee but I didn't. When I reached the fork I turned uproad and just kept riding.

In the years that followed I drifted a fair bit. I got myself on up to the Yellowstone and then went as far south as the Nueces. I moved around a lot and all the while I hoped I'd run onto him. When I'd ride into a place I hadn't been before I'd ask after him. I met fellers who'd known him before, back when he rode with spurs and wore a handgun on his hip. But I never found anyone who'd seen him since.

I worked a lot for other men and saved my money until finally I had stake enough to start this spread of my own. And in my travels I discovered there were a lot of girls as nice as Annie Johnson and Beth Ann Tatum. Some were even nicer, like the one I finally married.

It wasn't very long I'd been traveling when the white-face mare dropped a filly. And the old mare surprised me by rounding out and then dropping a he-colt. I kept the filly, gentling her the way Chino'd taught me. I bred both mares again to a good stud and both foaled again, though that was the last time for the old mare. Later I bred the filly too. In fact a good piece of my stake came from breeding and selling my own horses while I was working on beef ranches where the bosses didn't mind a hand doing a little business on his own.

But I always kept me a few brood mares with the Flag blood and I still do. Every horse I've got on this place is — well, at least part a Valdez horse.

That was the end of my story and when

I'd told it, the kid just sat there where he'd settled, looking wide-eyed at me. He was a bright, eager-looking youngun and I meant to hire him on and work him hard, if that was what he wanted.

I climbed down from the rail I'd been perched on and straightened up, feeling in my bones those twenty-five years that had passed since I was young and eager and just starting to work for Chino.

"Mister Wagner," the kid said, his voice soft and a little hoarse, "I come here apurpose. When I left home my pa told me to keep an eye out for sign of you. I'm Jamie Valdez."

The employees of Thorndike Press hope you have enjoyed this Large Print book. All our Large Print titles are designed for easy reading, and all our books are made to last. Other Thorndike Press Large Print books are available at your library, through selected bookstores, or directly from us.

For information about titles, please call:

(800) 257-5157

To share your comments, please write:

Publisher
Thorndike Press
P.O. Box 159
Thorndike, Maine 04986